HOT SUMMER KILLING

10P   2/76

HOT SUMMER KILLING

A Peter Styles Mystery Novel

BY JUDSON PHILIPS

LONDON
VICTOR GOLLANCZ LTD
1969

Printed in Great Britain by
Lowe & Brydone (Printers) Ltd., London

PART ONE

1

The boy pressed himself against the wall of the building, deep in the shadows, praying for invisibility, praying that the wall would open up and swallow him. Across the street they were slowly, methodically killing a man.

It had been going on for what seemed like forever. Timmy Fallon had been down in the East Village, the Hippie Village. There was a boy who played the guitar and sang. There were songs about freedom, and love, and lost children. Timmy had sat in a crowded, smoky room and listened and listened. It was suddenly after two in the morning and Timmy knew there was going to be hell to pay when he got home.

He had no particular concern about walking the ten blocks home alone. Nobody ever bothered a kid. It wasn't a good time of night for a rich-looking adult to be around alone. The desperate ones were apt to be prowling the streets; the ones who hadn't been able to find the money for the fix they'd needed all night. But they wouldn't bother a kid. A kid wouldn't have that kind of dough on him.

The bars had closed. The little shops on Third Avenue and

all along Timmy's route had iron grillwork shutters over their glass fronts. A few stray cats rummaged around garbage pails.

At Fourteenth Street Timmy headed west to Irving Place, and then uptown toward the apartment house near Gramercy Park where his father was custodian and where the Fallon family lived in a basement apartment.

Halfway between Fourteenth and Fifteenth Streets Timmy was attracted by a sound from the other side of the street. It was a voice, choked and breathless.

"Oh, please!" the voice said.

Timmy stopped and looked across the way. There were five men in a little group. Four of them surrounded the fifth man who stood, legs buckling under him, with his arms raised to cover his face and head. The four men, without any shouting or words, beat at the fifth man, slugged him in the stomach, pounded at him with fists like hammers, until slowly he sank down onto the pavement. Suddenly the four men seemed to evaporate. Into alleys? Into doorways? Timmy couldn't tell. Only the man sprawled on the pavement remained.

A taxi rolled swiftly up Irving Place. If the driver or the passenger in the taxi had seen the man on the pavement, they ignored him.

Slowly, the man struggled up onto his hands and knees, shaking his head like a punch-drunk fighter.

"Oh, please!" he moaned.

Timmy's impulse was to help, but somehow he couldn't make himself move away from the shadow of the buildings on his side of the street. But he started up town, keeping pace with the distressed man. It was a hot August night and sweat ran down inside Timmy's clothes.

Suddenly, from nowhere, the four men appeared again. No

words, no angry shouts—just machine-like violence as they beat their victim down to the pavement again. This time, once he was down, the four men kicked at him, viciously, cruelly. Timmy could hear the low, anguished moan from the beaten man.

Then once again the four men evaporated. The beaten man was a pile of dark rags on the sidewalk.

Timmy looked around. He knew this neighborhood like the back of his hand. Pete's Bar would be closed, and the paper store, and the man in the parking garage would be asleep somewhere in the upper regions, responsive only to the night bell. In one or two of the taller buildings he saw lights. He thought of shouting at the top of his lungs for help, and knew, as he thought of it, that he couldn't make a sound. Where was a cop? There was never a cop when you needed one.

The dark rags on the other side of the street moved again. The man dragged himself up and staggered northward. At the corner of Seventeenth Street the four men waited.

The hunted man turned, took one running step, and fell. The four men were on him. A street light showed Timmy a broken bottle in one of the men's hands. Jagged edges of glass smashed down into the fallen man's face.

There was a terrible scream.

That scream seemed to throw off Timmy's paralysis. He ran toward home. There was a shout, and glancing over his shoulder he saw that one of the four men had taken off after him. Timmy cut east on Eighteenth Street and cut again into a narrow alley. This alley had been his playground as a very small boy. At the end of it was a high board fence that surrounded a garden apartment. His one chance was to get over that fence before his pursuer came into view.

3

Timmy had made that leap before. In the pitch darkness his judgement of distance was accurate. A bounding leap took him up so that his hands gripped the top of the fence. He scrambled up and fell over on the other side into a soft flower bed. He lay there, choking back the urge to sob out his terror. On the other side of the fence he heard swift, powerful feet running down the alley—and past!

"You will come straight toward the house with your hands up," a cold voice said, "or I'll shoot you down without a moment's hesitation."

"Oh, Peter!" Timmy cried.

A light went on in the garden apartment. A man stood framed in the French doors. He was wearing undershorts and a T-shirt. He stood on one leg, because his right leg was missing below the knee. He leaned against the door jamb to balance himself. In his right hand was a gun, steady as a rock.

"You damned little idiot," the man said. "Don't you know I might have blown your head off without warning you?"

"Oh, Peter!" Timmy cried out, scrambling toward the figure in the doorway. "They're killing a man out there!" . . .

Peter Styles sat on the edge of his bed, adjusting the harness that fastened on his artificial leg, a thing of aluminum and plastic and magical springs that created an ankle joint. The bedside phone was cradled over a hunched shoulder.

"Sergeant Conway?" Peter's voice was crisp. "Peter Styles here . . . I'm fine, but no time to talk about the weather . . . Three or four men are beating another guy to death out on Irving Place . . . No, I haven't seen it, but a kid in the building here has just told me about it. I'm on my way

4

out . . . Don't worry. I can take care of myself."

Timmy Fallon spilled out his story as Peter pulled on slacks, a turtleneck white knit shirt, and a tweed jacket.

"You recognize any of the men, Timmy? You know everyone in this neighborhood."

"The street lights aren't too bright along Irving Place," Timmy said. "Not with all the stores and places closed. They—they weren't beatnik types. Big strong guys with short haircuts—like work clothes. I don't ever remember seeing them. The one who chased me—I'd know him if I saw him again. I could never forget him."

"And the man they're attacking?"

"He's a Negro, Peter. Nicely dressed—or was before they started tearing at him."

"God!" Peter said. He slipped the gun into the pocket of his tweed coat. They had been promised a long hot summer by the more violent elements of the Black Power complex, but so far nothing had happened to ignite the fuse that would set off an explosion of violence and terror in the city.

At the door of the apartment, Peter paused to take a heavy blackthorn walking stick out of a crockery umbrella stand. In the days when he had first begun to learn how to use his artificial leg the blackthorn had been a balancing tool. He took it now as a weapon.

"I want you to stay here, Timmy," Peter said to the boy. "Call your father on the telephone and tell him what's happened. But don't go anywhere unless your father or I come for you."

"Can't I go with you, Peter?"

"I don't want the man who chased you to see you again," Peter said. "Do as I tell you."

To the several million Americans who read *Newsview*

Magazine, Peter Styles is a familiar personality. His weekly column in the magazine is one of its prime features. His personal story accounts for much of what has made him famous as a commentator on the senseless violence of our times. Some five years before that night in Irving Place, Peter had been returning from a Vermont ski lodge in his car with his father. Two laughing hoodlums had played tag with them coming down the winding mountain road and Peter's car had suddenly crashed through a guard rail and somersaulted down into a deep valley. Peter had been thrown clear. In his last conscious moment, he heard his father screaming for help Peter couldn't give him as he was burned alive in the wreckage. Peter came to in a hospital minus his right leg below the knee.

It had taken a long time for him to recover physically and psychologically from that tragic accident. But he had made it. His style as a writer had changed from that of a light and witty observer of the social scene into a white hot crusader against the meaningless violences that seemed to be a creeping sickness involving the country.

New York City, where he had lived all his life and which he loved, had changed. People were frankly afraid to walk the quieter streets at night. Only a few blocks from his apartment off Irving Place, teenagers in the East Village were involved with drugs, rape, and murder. During the long hot summer tensions were high. There had been riots in other cities, and New York waited, scarcely daring to breathe, praying that there would be no bloodshed or mass destruction of property. The voices of underprivileged people crying for help and recognition were loud and angry. It would take only the smallest incident to set off a powder keg of terror. That incident, Peter sensed, might be just beyond his front doorstep.

6

He walked with an almost undiscernible limp, the blackthorn stick tucked under his arm. The city was quiet. At the corner of Irving Place he encountered a middle-aged woman tugging at an arthritic spaniel on a leash.

"Thank God!" the woman said. "There's a man on the sidewalk across Irving Place. I—I think he's badly hurt. I didn't know what to do. I—I had my dog!"

Peter didn't pause. He walked toward what Timmy had described as a "bundle of rags" on the other side of Irving Place. There was no one in sight except the whimpering woman, behind him, with the dog. Sergeant Conway had not yet answered his phone call.

Peter's breath made a rasping sound in his throat as he looked down at the Negro man on the pavement. He didn't need an ambulance intern to tell him that there was nothing to be done. It was too late for help. Eyes were rolled up into the man's head, and the black face was brutally slashed, probably by the broken bottle Timmy had mentioned. An arm was twisted crookedly under the body, clearly broken. The mouth was cut and swollen, and jagged, broken teeth grinned up at Peter through a red froth.

The woman with the dog edged forward, watching the slender, dark man with the blackthorn stick. His mouth was a straight, hard line. His pale, cold blue eyes seemed to darken with compassion.

"I—I could call a doctor from my apartment," the woman said.

"Thanks, but it's no use," Peter said. He turned away, a little shudder running over him. "Poor devil. I know who he is." . . .

A red light blinked on the roof of the police patrol car that pulled up at the curb beside Peter. Two patrolmen got out, one of them with a drawn gun. The first one recognized Peter, who was well known in the area. There had been a time when the men of the local precinct had been on a round-the-clock surveillance of Peter and his apartment, protecting him against a threatened rub-out by friends of a man who was spending the rest of his life in prison because of Peter's activities.

"Evening, Mr. Styles. Sergeant Conway said it was you phoned in."

"Hello, Powalski."

The second man, the one with the drawn gun, looked up from the body on the pavement. "We need the meat wagon," he said. He went over to the patrol car and began tinkering with the two-way radio. A scratchy answering voice seemed distastefully loud.

"You saw it happen?" Patrolman Powalski asked Peter.

Peter shook his head. "Mike Fallon's kid, Tim—you know Mike; custodian of half a dozen small buildings around here—came scrambling over the wall into my garden. He was being chased by one of the men who did this."

"Kid up at this time of night?"

"He'd been to some kind of love-in downtown." Peter told Timmy's story, just the facts.

"Can't identify?"

"No. But I know who the dead man is. His name is Richard Sims. He was one of the bright young Negro intellectuals. Has a play running off-Broadway right now, I think. *Sound The Dark Trumpet*."

"There was some kind of a mass meeting down around Union Square," Powalski said. "We were alerted in case the lid blew off. Hot summer. This guy might have been there."

8

"It was four white men who killed him."

"And how many black men will now set out to kill those four white men, and use it as an excuse to destroy how much property and kill how many cops?" Powalski asked, bitterly.

"You need me any longer?" Peter asked.

"They'll want to talk to the kid."

"Can't you leave him out of it? The man who chased him may not have gotten a good look at him. He was running in the shadows. You call him in openly, you may finger him for a kill. They won't want a witness to what they did."

"I'll say that to the Captain. He'll play it close to the vest, I'd guess."

Peter walked around the corner to The Players, the club where he spent a good deal of his city leisure time. The graceful old house, given as a club for actors and men in the allied arts by the famous Edwin Booth, was dark except for a small glow through the opaque glass top on the inner door. Peter rang the night bell. After a while Tommy, the night doorman, appeared.

"Sorry to keep you waiting, Mr. Styles. I was on the third floor."

"Sorry to bother you. I wanted to look at your phone book. A man's been killed out around the corner."

"It isn't safe anymore anywhere," Tommy said.

Peter went down the sharp flight of stairs to the dimly lit grillroom, past the pool table to the telephone booths. He switched on the light over the telephone books, studied the Manhattan directory for a moment, and then went back up the stairs to the foyer.

"Where is the best place to hope for a taxi this time of night, Tommy?"

"Cafeteria around Twenty-fifth and Fourth Avenue,"

Tommy said. "Drivers stop there for a coffee-and."

"Thanks." Peter started for the door.

"Watch your step, Mr. Styles. Your man who got killed; I suppose it was some junkie trying to raise the price of a fix?"

"I doubt it," Peter said. "See you around, Tommy."

Peter had luck. He picked up a cruising taxi when he'd gone just across Gramercy Park. He gave the driver an address in the West Seventies. The taxi had a radio that was picking up police calls. Peter glanced at the license information in the rack in front of him. Patrick Clancy.

"How come the police calls?" Peter asked.

Clancy looked up into his rear view mirror. "I'm moonlighting," he said.

"You're a cop?"

"Fifteenth Precinct," Clancy said. "I heard some guy got knocked off on Irving Place. That's how I happened to be in the neighborhood. Nothing I could do. How come you're going to this fleabag?"

"Fleabag?"

"The address you give me. Hotel Molyneaux. Call girls. Queers. You're Peter Styles, aren't you?"

"Yes."

"Recognized you from the picture they use in *Newsview*. Saw you limp a little when you walked toward my cab. Like your stuff."

"Thanks. So the address I gave you is a hotel?"

"You didn't know?"

"Looked up a man's address in the phone book. It just gave a street number."

"If he's an okay guy, he wouldn't want anyone to know he was living at the Molyneaux," Clancy said.

Fleabag was an apt description for the Molyneaux. There was a dilapidated iron and glass awning out over the sidewalk. The letter "y" was missing from the peeling gold sign on the front of that awning. Inside, the lobby was dirty, dimly lit. An ancient clerk with an old fashioned green eyeshade on his forehead was reading a comic book at the desk.

"Richard Sims, please," Peter said.

"Four-o-two," the clerk said, without looking up. He waved vaguely toward a self-service elevator across the way.

The elevator creaked up to the fourth floor. Peter hesitated outside the door of 402 and then knocked. A moment later the door was opened a few inches, a chain on the inside stopping it. A pretty but tired-looking blond girl looked at Peter. Her skin was milk white.

"Mrs. Sims?" Peter asked.

"Yes."

"I wonder if I could talk to you for a moment. My name is Peter Styles."

"Oh my God, something's happened to Richard!" the girl said.

"I'm afraid so."

"How bad?"

"The very worst, I'm afraid."

The door was closed abruptly in his face—and then reopened without the inhibiting chain. The blond girl clung to the doorknob as though she needed it for support.

"It was at the meeting?" the girl asked. "I begged him not to go. I pleaded with him not to go. Sprague and the others were ready to take off. He knew it. He knew they'd turn on him."

"Perhaps you'd better sit down," Peter said.

The room was a surprise. There were two windows looking out over a dark air shaft and directly at a blank brick wall. But the room itself was lined with books from floor to ceiling. There was a large center work table with a typewriter, neatly covered with a plastic dust protector. There was a couch and two comfortable overstuffed chairs. Peter guessed that the couch opened up into a bed. It was neat and clean. There were lamps that provided a soft light.

The blond Mrs. Sims moved vaguely back into the room like someone feeling her way in the dark.

"It was at the meeting?" she asked.

"No." Peter had managed to keep his surprise completely under control. He hadn't known that Richard Sims was married to a white girl. "He was walking up town—Irving Place—about an hour ago. A young boy in the neighborhood saw him being attacked by four men. He came to me for help. By the time I got to your husband it was too late."

"Oh my God!"

"I came here to prepare you for what is going to happen any minute now. The police."

The girl turned, her mouth a bitter, crooked line. "And to get what from me first? Oh, I know who you are, Mr. Styles. A high-priced newspaperman." She turned away again. "I'm sorry. You're just doing your job. Richard was an advocate of a non-violent revolt. Jack Sprague and his Black Power crowd hated him. He could be persuasive. He knew how to use words. He went to the meeting tonight because he knew it could be explosive. Oh, I know you and your crowd, Mr. Styles. You've editorialized in your magazine about Richard. One of the 'few sane people' in the Negro movement, you've called him. Oh my God, Mr. Styles, have you ever heard anyone approve of non-violence, except when a black man proposes it?" She shook her head from side to side. "Richard! Oh, Richard!"

"He was killed by four white men, Mrs. Sims. Not Sprague or any of his crowd."

She turned, slowly. Her eyes were wide as saucers. "I killed him!" she whispered.

"My dear woman—"

"*I killed him!*" Her voice rose hysterically. "I should never have married him. Everything has gone wrong for him ever since. His people hate him because of me. My people hate him. I should have turned my back on him. I should have run when he asked me. But oh my God, I loved him so!"

There was a sharp knock on the door of the hotel room.

"Try to get hold of yourself," Peter said.

"Mrs. Sims!" The knock was repeated.

The girl made a helpless little gesture and Peter went to the door and opened it. There were two men outside the door and one of them was a startling surprise to Peter. He was a stocky, grey-haired man with mild grey eyes. A charred black briar pipe dangled from one corner of his mouth. He was Jerome Marshall, Manhattan's District Attorney. The D.A. never shows up in person at a homicide investigation; not at the early preliminaries.

"Hello, Peter," Jerry Marshall said. They knew each other from way back. "Glad to find you here." The mild grey eyes went past Peter to the girl, who had gripped the back of an armchair to steady herself. "I'm Jerome Marshall, Mrs. Sims, the District Attorney. And this is Lieutenant Pike of the Homicide Squad."

Pike was a big, burly man with a fringe of red hair around a bald head. He turned and closed the door. He looked

13

embarrassed.

"Peter's broken the news to you," Marshall said.

The girl nodded.

"I'm sorry; genuinely, deeply sorry."

"That won't bring him back." She shook her head from side to side. "He'd scold me for using such a cliché. You—you can't think of anything original to say at a time like this."

"I understand," Marshall said. He frowned at his pipe as though he was surprised to find it out of tobacco. He reached into the hip pocket of his grey tweed trousers and produced a yellow oilskin pouch. "You may not know that it's rather unusual for me to be present at the early stages of an investigation. Peter knows. He was surprised to see me."

"You're here because you're afraid this may set off a violence," the girl said.

Jerome Marshall had held the District Attorney's job for a good many years, supported by both political parties. His integrity as a public official was a by-word. His judgments of people, honest and dishonest, were almost invariably sound. He could be a very grim guardian of the law and of people's rights under it. He was, instinctively, a man of sympathy, compassion, with something like a psychiatrist's understanding of the intolerable pressures that drive the human animal to anti-social extremes.

"There are times, Mrs. Sims," Marshall said, "when our job is most distasteful. We are forced to come at people in tragic moments like this, forced to disregard their need to be alone to pull themselves together, to put on an invulnerable face for the public, the press." He glanced at Peter. "Have you anyone to help you, Mrs. Sims? Family? A lawyer? Friends of your husband's?"

14

"My husband's friends will flush me down the drain with an enormous sense of relief." She laughed. It was a little too high-pitched. "I was the white sheep of the family; the white mark on Richard's record. I think—I think they killed him because he believed what he said and lived by his belief. There are no white people and black people; only good people and bad people."

"Your own family?"

"I have a sister who speaks to me. I'm dead as far as the rest of them are concerned."

"Would you like to call your sister?"

The girl hesitated and then she shook her head. "Let Carol read about it in the paper. Then she can make up her own mind whether she wants to be with me or not. She won't be faced with responding one way or the other to a cry for help."

Marshall held a lighter to his pipe and blew out a cloud of smoke. "Suppose she doesn't read it in the paper?" he asked.

"Then a thousand well-wishers will call her to say, 'Have you read the news about Marian's husband?'"

"Suppose," Marshall said, in an oddly quiet voice, watching the smoke from his pipe float away across the room, "—suppose her friends don't read it in the paper?"

"Now wait a minute, Jerry—" Peter said.

Marshall drew a deep breath. He suddenly sounded tired and old. "I want forty-eight hours, Peter," he said. "That's why I'm here. To ask you, Peter—to ask Mrs. Sims."

"You want to suppress the story?" Peter asked, not believing.

"For forty-eight hours."

"It's impossible," Peter said. "There's young Tim Fallon."

15

"There's an assistant of mine with the Fallons now," Marshall said, "persuading them that the boy will be in grave danger if they don't keep their mouths shut."

"There are the four men who killed him."

"They may be puzzled, but are they likely to complain?" Marshall asked. "Of course if they do, we've got 'em."

"There was a woman with an old spaniel dog."

Marshall nodded. "It's my experience that coincidences rarely work in my favor," he said. "In this instance—the woman happens to be the mother of one of my office staff." Marshall's pipe had gone out again and he looked at it, almost stupidly. "That leaves you and Mrs. Sims."

"Why?" Peter asked.

"He's afraid, if the story breaks, that the long hot summer will get under way full blast," Marian Sims said. "You want time for the Governor to organize the National Guard, Mr. Marshall?" The edge of bitterness was so sharp it hurt. "You people always play for a special advantage. We—because I think of myself as Negro, Mr. Marshall—are always asked to give you do-gooders a special advantage, so you can slap us down."

"A fair accusation I think, Mrs. Sims," Marshall said. He tried to get his pipe going again. "Have you ever seen total panic in a big city? I saw it in Paris in World War Two as the Germans came close for the first time. Thousands of people trying to get away—anywhere, anyhow; struggling with each other for space on any kind of transportation available; sick with terror."

"Oh my God, Mr. Marshall, do we have to take this time to discuss the logistics of riot? My husband is dead!"

"Please bear with me, Mrs. Sims," Marshall said. "I have a

16

human responsibility to you. I have a legal responsibility to eight million people. I have no choice except to ignore your personal anguish, to ask you some questions, to tell you half a truth—and then ask you a favor which you have to grant."

"And if I refuse?" Marian Sims asked.

"Then your cooperation will, of necessity, become involuntary," Marshall said.

"This is the damndest thing I ever heard of," Peter said, anger beginning to simmer. "Will my cooperation also be involuntary, Jerry?"

"I hope not," Marshall said. He walked over toward the dark window that looked out at a brick wall.

"You don't have to answer questions without legal advice, Mrs. Sims," Lieutenant Pike said, speaking for the first time. His deep voice sounded like distant thunder.

"I'm aware of that," Marian Sims said. "So I will not answer what I choose not to answer."

She was astonishing, Peter thought. Faced with tragedy, she had the courage to stand her ground, to fight back against what must seem to her to be the enemy.

"Did your husband ever tell you about a key plan for this summer's rebellion by the Negro community?" Pike asked.

"There were a dozen plans, a thousand plans," Marian Sims answered promptly. "That's our problem. We are all chiefs and no Indians."

"I'm talking about something more specific than a riot, set off, let us say, by something like your husband's death."

"Why do you worry about riots, Mr. Pike?" Marian asked. "Who gets killed? A few cops and thousands of Negroes. Whose property is burned by the rioters? The property of other Negroes. Whose stores are looted? The stores owned by other Negroes. Why do you care? Why not let us destroy ourselves? Wouldn't that be easier for you?"

"You yourself said a little while ago this wasn't a good time to discuss logistics?" Pike said. His grin was boyish. It disappeared and his whole face seemed to scowl. "We think, Mrs. Sims, that there is a specific plan to hit the city and hit it hard. Did your husband ever mention it?"

"No. No special plan. Sprague screams we should burn down Madison Square Garden, burn down Columbia University, burn down Gracie Mansion. Richard and others urge that we should protest on a large scale—a scale that would be felt and understood—but without violence. But Richard never mentioned any special plan to me."

"Thank you," Pike said. "This is Wednesday morning." He glanced at his wrist watch. "Ten minutes to five. We believe that on Friday, at about five in the afternoon—that's roughly sixty hours—this special plan will be set in motion. We need time, Mrs. Sims, to get ready for it. If the news of your husband's death breaks this morning, say, it may set off a chain reaction that will trigger this plan before we are ready to defend against it. Simple as that."

"It doesn't sound simple at all," Marian Sims said.

"Sprague and your husband disagreed," Pike said. "But Sprague will make a hero of your husband and use his death to set off his explosion."

"My husband was a hero," Marian said, quietly.

Jerry Marshall came slowly back from the window. He was rubbing the bowl of his pipe against the side of his nose. "It would take courage, Mrs. Sims," he said. "Perhaps more courage than we have a right to ask of you."

Shrewd old bastard, Peter thought. Suggest to this girl that

18

she didn't have enough courage for a given situation and she'd take on King Kong.

"What kind of courage?" Marian asked.

"You'd have to live for two days as though nothing had happened," Marshall said. "If people ask about your husband, you'll have to act as though he is all right—a trip somewhere. You'll have to lie to your family, your friends, your husband's family and friends."

"And if the story breaks? If it leaks to some newspaper—or the radio, or television?"

"Then we've lost," Marshall said, with a weary shrug. "We'd ask nothing further of you." His tired eyes looked at her with an intense directness. "The lives of a great many thousands of innocent people may depend on our being able to keep the lid on things for a few days."

"What about Richard's people? The Negro people. Will I be doing them a service, or betraying them? Can you answer that honestly, Mr. Marshall?"

"I believe that if we can circumvent this special plan Pike's mentioned, you'll be doing them a favor," Marshall said. "If this thing is triggered before we're ready to handle it, I believe there could be a slaughter of Negroes, not only here but all over the country, that would make Hitler's pogrom against the Jews look like a kindergarten game of tag." The District Attorney's voice was low and impassioned.

"How can I believe that?"

"If twenty-five thousand people, most of them white, were to be wiped off the face of the earth in the next ten minutes as the result of an extremist Negro plot, what do you think would happen, Mrs. Sims? I think that not a single Negro in the country would find his life worth a plugged nickel."

Marian Sims stood, still clinging to the back of her chair,

chewing on her lower lip. "And you think the news of Richard's murder could start all this happening?"

"It could," Marshall said.

"Mind you, Mrs. Sims," Pike said, "we don't say it can't be triggered some other way, by some other incident. But every policeman and every law officer in this city is on the alert. That's how Mr. Marshall was ready to come here the moment we heard about Mr. Sims."

"You're not telling me enough," Marian Sims said.

"I'm telling you all I can, Mrs. Sims."

You looked at Marshall and listened to him and you had to believe him.

"I don't know why, but I'll do what you ask," the girl said, in a very small voice.

Pike was writing something on a page of his pocket notebook. When he'd finished he tore out the page and handed it to Marian Sims.

"We can't protect you openly, Mrs. Sims," he said. "By that I mean I can't station a man here in your room or in the hallway or the lobby. It could arouse suspicion. But there will be help very close by. If you feel frightened by anything, by any approach that's made to you, call this number. There'll be someone here in five minutes."

"What am I supposed to be afraid of?" Marian asked.

"Your husband just may have been killed because he knew too much about something," Pike said. "If he knew, it could be supposed that you know. Someone may have recognized us when we came here—or Mr. Styles. That could arouse suspicion."

"What have you done with Richard?" Her voice had gone dead.

"I promise you, Mrs. Sims," Marshall said, "that he's being

handled gently and with respect."

Marian walked unsteadily to the couch and sat down. Her hand stroked the seat cushion beside her. Richard's place?

"I'll do it, Mr. Marshall," she said, "with the understanding that after Friday you'll tell me the whole truth."

"I promise—or at least I promise that you'll know, whether I tell it to you or it just happens."

"I want the explanation from you, Mr. Marshall!"

"I might not be able."

"Why? Someone can keep you silent?"

"Yes. You see, I could be dead, Mrs. Sims."

2

Outside the Hotel Molyneaux on the sidewalk the sky in the east was blood red.

" 'Red in the morning, sailor take warning—' " Marshall said, softly.

A limousine came along the curb and stopped. Pike opened the rear door. "See you later, Mr. Marshall. I'll be at headquarters."

"Thanks, Pike. Thanks for being persuasive."

"Lot of guts that girl has."

"A lot," Marshall said. "Get in, Peter."

"Just a minute," Peter said. "I have a story that needs filing with my news service. The story of a murder and the curious antics of the District Attorney to suppress it."

"Oh, you're not going to file that story, Peter," Marshall said. "You're coming to my apartment for breakfast and I'm going to persuade you not to."

"How?"

Marshall gave him a tired smile. "Why, by telling you whole truth, of course. I wouldn't insult you with anything less than that."

"You'll go along when you hear it, Mr. Styles," Pike said.

Peter's curiosity was too great to refuse. It wasn't as though he was working for a daily paper with a late morning edition coming up. He realized that he had until the following Monday to do a complete story for *Newsview*, a weekly magazine, on the night's tragedy and its strange political overtones. If anyone but Jerome Marshall himself had dealt with Marian Sims in such wildly melodramatic terms, Peter wouldn't have listened for a minute. Marshall's usual technique was to underplay, not to embroider.

"You'll find messages for you all over town," Marshall said, leaning back against the car's upholstery, his eyes closed. "When I got the word that you were the one who'd turned in the alarm on Sims I was desperate to find you."

"You're using an awful lot of five-dollar words tonight, Jerry. Words like 'desperate.' "

"It's that kind of situation." Marshall opened his eyes to look at Peter. "What took you to see Mrs. Sims?"

"Impulse. The Fallon boy's description of what happened was pretty horrible. I guessed what the uproar would be. I thought the man's wife needed a chance to prepare herself for the avalanche of police and reporters."

"Unusually sympathetic attitude."

"I'd heard Sims speak on a number of occasions. I'd read a lot of his stuff—poetry, two novels, articles in the Negro press and magazines. He struck me as a sensitive, warm, tender person. No fanatic. That kind of man is usually married to that kind of woman. And I felt indirectly guilty."

"Guilty?"

"White men killed him," Peter said.

"Did you know about her?"

"That she was white? No. I wonder why I didn't. There's been enough written about him."

Jerome Marshall had lived on Central Park West, not too far from the Molyneaux, for many years. His two sons had grown up there. They'd both gone to college in the city. One of them had died a year ago in the jungles of Vietnam. The other was an electronics engineer for some big outfit. Marshall and his wife, Betty, were grandparents. The Central Park West apartment was too large for just the two of them, but it had been home for so long they didn't want to be practical and give it up.

Betty Marshall met them at the front door. She was a tall, dark, handsome woman who at fifty-five had kept the figure much admired when she was twenty-five. She was a warm friendly person who had devoted her life to making the going pleasant and as easy as possible for her husband and sons. The Marshalls were an anachronism, Peter thought, as he saw Betty kiss her husband's cheek as she took his hat from him and gave Peter a welcoming smile. Two gentle, quiet people whose whole lives had been entwined with the most vicious criminality in the city's life.

"I see you found Peter," Betty Marshall said. "There's coffee ready. I can have toast and eggs in five minutes. There's some very good Danish."

"Just coffee, darling," Marshall said. "Peter may be hungrier than I am."

"Just coffee, thanks," Peter said. "Black."

"Any luck with Mrs. Sims?" Betty asked.

"I think." Marshall smiled. "Now I have to have some luck with Peter."

24

"Oh, Peter!" Betty Marshall said.

"You say that as though I was a pushover," Peter said, resenting it just a little.

"My dear Peter, not a pushover, just a very reasonable, sensible man."

"In my study, if it's all right," Marshall said.

"Of course, darling. There've been about a hundred phone calls. I followed orders. You were out. I didn't know when you'd be back. I didn't bother to write down the names—except one. Hizzoner the Mayor!"

"I'll call him when I finish with Peter," Marshall said. "I'm still 'out' until I finish with Peter."

Down a short corridor was Marshall's study. It was a large, plainly furnished room with windows looking out over the park. Most of the rest of the wall space was filled with a calf-bound law library. On a flat-topped desk were three telephone instruments, a tape recorder, and a small portable television set.

"I don't spend my time watching *Mission Impossible*," Marshall said, with a tired smile, "although you may think so before I get through with you. I listen to the politicians and the rabble rousers; the people who'd like to have my hide." He sat down behind the desk and gestured to a green leather armchair.

Peter sat down, stretching out his artificial leg with a little wince of pain. He'd been standing on it a long time. Betty Marshall appeared almost at once with a tray holding coffee cups and an electric percolator. She plugged the pot into a connection in the floor beside the desk.

"Drink hearty," she said, and was gone.

Peter took a sip of coffee. It was hot and good. "Wonderful woman, Betty," he said. "This rat race of yours never stops and she never seems flustered."

"We're all a little flustered tonight," Marshall said. He took a manila folder out of the center desk drawer. Glasses came from the breast pocket of his tweed jacket. He opened the folder and looked at papers for a moment. Then he handed one of them across to Peter.

"A photostat," he said.

It was a letter addressed to Mr. Martin Severance, Commissioner of Transportation, City Hall, New York.

It began abruptly:

Listen Severance

You wanted something to show the bigwigs. Here it is. Unless ten million dollars in unmarked and untracable money is in our hands by noon on Friday the 23rd of August we act. If you don't deliver we will, at five o'clock, at the height of the commuter rush, blow Grand Central Station off the city map. We don't guaranty that the Pan Am building won't come toppling down into the wreckage.

There is no room for bargaining. Those are our terms.

Black Power

Peter looked up from the photostat, frowning. "Kid stuff. Crackpot," he said.

Marshall nodded, as if to say he'd told himself that over and over again. "Let me give you the history of it. About three weeks ago, Severance got a phone call at his home in Beekman Place. You know Marty Severance?"

"Who he is," Peter said. "One of the Mayor's special appointees, isn't he?"

"Classmate of the Mayor's at Princeton," Marshall said.

"Very Ivy League. Bright, cultivated, tough character. Moneyed background. Doesn't scare easily. Done a remarkably good job with the whole transportation mess in the city."

"So he got a phone call."

"I'll give it to you—a little free hand. Marty made a tape for me." Marshall reached forward and pressed a button on his recorder. The tape spools began to turn. A clear pleasant voice began:

"The call came at eleven forty-five on July thirty-first," Severance's voice said. "I checked the time when he'd been talking about twenty seconds. I suspected it was trouble.

" 'Severance?' he said, when I answered.

" 'Yes.'

" 'Been a nice cool summer, wouldn't you say?'

"I knew what he meant. It was a Negro voice. I agreed that it had been a nice cool summer.

" 'Time's up, Severance. Things are gonna turn hot.'

" 'You're warning me of riots to come?'

"He laughed. 'Riots are old fashioned, Mr. Martin, sir. We're gonna be more direct. We're gonna make our point clearer.'

" 'How?' I asked him.

" 'There's a lot of big talk about poverty programs and rebuilding the slums and civil rights and all that horseshit,' he said. 'We've decided the only way for anything to happen is for us to have the money in our own hands to spend on our own people. Let the bureaucrats go screw themselves. We want the money in our own sweaty little hands.'

" 'I agree you might handle it better than some of our government agencies,' I said.

" 'Glad you agree, because I'm calling to tell you we want

27

ten millions bucks, and you're the boy who'll get it for us, Mr. Martin, sir.'

" 'Wish I could. But you're joking of course.'

" 'Not joking, dad. Not joking at all. Now you cool it while I tell you. Ten million bucks in our hands by noon on the twenty-third of August. Ten million bucks in unmarked bills—or else.'

" 'Or else what?'

" 'Or else at five o'clock that night we blow up Grand Central Station with all the people in it. Some other real estate may come tumbling down in the process. Say the Pan-Am Building.'

" 'You're talking crazy.'

" 'I'm telling you, Mr. Martin, sir.'

" 'Why have you chosen to tell me this?'

" 'Because you suck around the Mayor more than most, Mr. Martin, sir, and he's the one will have to get the money up.'

" 'He'll laugh at me when I tell him about this phone call. Because it's crazy. You know that.'

" 'I'll put it on paper for you to show to him.'

" 'And how do I reach you with his answer?'

"He laughed. 'I reach you, Mr. Martin, sir. Once every twenty four hours I reach you. That is, until noon on the twenty-third of August. After that it's too late and I don't reach you. Then, at five o'clock, voom! No more station. No more trains in and out of the city. Twenty to thirty thousand dead commuters and bystanders. Then we get in touch again and tell you what the next target will be.'

"He sounded crazy, but I was scared. 'Okay, you call me here tomorrow, this same time, and I'll tell you what the Mayor has to say.'

28

"He laughed again. 'I call you here, this same time, and your phone is tapped, and twenty-five of the fuzz are listening in, ready to trace where I'm calling from. No, no. I'll know where you are, Mr. Martin, sir, every minute of every day and night. I'll get in touch when I know it's safe to get in touch. Good night, Mr. Martin, sir—you sonofabitch.' "

The spools on the tape recorder kept turning but there was no more sound. Marshall leaned forward and pressed the cutoff button. He looked at Peter and waited.

"It's somebody trying to scare you, and you've all evidently bought it," Peter said.

"It's not a new idea," Marshall said. "The Black Power hierarchy has been talking about it for the past year. Mrs. Sims made the point for us, Peter. Who gets killed in the riots? Other Negroes. Whose property gets destroyed? The property of other Negroes. So maybe a few white cops get killed, and some people on the fringe areas get roughed up, scared, and batten down their hatches. The riots destroy the people the rioters are, theoretically, demonstrating for. A new concept has been talked about quite openly. It's been said on radio and television panel shows that go into millions of homes. Nobody really believes it. The point is, however, that the white community can only be made to pay attention to the Black community, if they are hit where they live."

"It would make tactical sense," Peter said.

"My staff has been getting wind of it here and there for a long time," Marshall said. "The one thing that's stopped it so far is organized leadership. I quote Mrs. Sims again, 'We're all chiefs and no Indians.' Perhaps, here in New York, a leadership has taken charge."

"This kooky phone call and the letter convince you of that?" Peter asked.

"Not by themselves," Marshall said. "I reacted as you did. Crackpot melodrama."

"They warn you three weeks in advance," Peter said. "You have cops, your staff, the FBI. How can they get away with it when you're sitting there waiting for it—prepared?"

"That's what I said." Marshall drew a deep breath. "Two weeks ago—a week after the phone call—we had a bomb scare at Grand Central."

"Just a minute. Did Martin Severance hear from this man every day, as promised?"

"He did. He was phoned every day. At his office; in the middle of a business luncheon; at a nightclub where he was spending the evening; at an airport where he was taking off for Washington. Once every twenty-four hours. Never in the same place. Always repeating the threat and demanding an answer." .

"I see. So you had a bomb scare."

"They're not infrequent. Calls saying there's a bomb in a building, or in the luggage on a plane at Kennedy; or in a locker in the subway. Nine times out of ten they're a complete false alarm. Once in ten there is something, usually a home-made gadget; often quite lethal if they went off in a plane, or in a small area."

"And this one at Grand Central?"

"A call saying there was a bomb in one of the pay toilets under the Commodore Hotel. You can imagine we were a little edgy. The bomb squad was on the scene in ten minutes. They found a bomb. It was in a large suitcase. It was a complex, highly sophisticated mechanism. Nothing home-made about it. It was a warhead that might well have fitted on an aerial bomb. It had an explosive capacity equal to hundreds of tons of TNT." Marshall's voice shook slightly. "It could

30

have done the job they're talking about pretty effectively."

"You're serious?"

"Perfectly serious. There was something missing from this bomb, though. There was no firing mechanism. It would never have gone off. City and military experts took it apart. It was foolproof, deadly. If it had been exploded—the hotel, the station, God knows how much more, would have been a shambles. Scotch-taped to the bomb was a note."

"Don't tell me. I can guess," Peter said. Color seemed to have drained from his face.

Marshall nodded. "It said, simply: 'August twenty-third. Five P.M.'"

Peter got up from his chair and moved restlessly across the room. He took a black shellbriar pipe from his pocket, but he didn't fill it or light it. He stood by the window, tapping the empty bowl in the palm of his hand. Daylight was spreading over Central Park. It was going to be a hot, humid day.

"As you can imagine," Marshall said, his voice monotonous with fatigue, "we had to be convinced."

Peter turned sharply from the window. "And so you are all involved in what we used to call 'brinksmanship.'"

Marshall nodded, his eyelids heavy.

"The Mayor?"

"He refuses to submit to extortion," Marshall said.

"Who else knows?"

"The City Council. The Police Commissioner. Some special men on the force, like Pike. Half a dozen carefully selected assistants of mine. The bomb squad detail. The White House and whoever has been informed from there. The FBI."

"But not the public. Not the press."

"No. You stumbled on it in a way, Peter. You're the one

31

and only."

"Because I found Sims dead on Irving Place?"

"Because we're deathly afraid something may trigger this thing before the deadline. To keep you still about Sims, I've taken it on myself to tell you the whole story."

"But before twelve o'clock on Friday the money will be paid?"

Marshall shrugged. "I don't know what the decision will be, Peter. It's not mine to make. Until the deadline it's my job to try to find Martin Severance's phone chum."

"What would happen if this went out on television and radio in the next ten minutes?" Peter asked.

"Panic," Marshall said. "Panic and unbelievable violence. Thousands of people would try to get out of the city. It would be like the news that a Russian hydrogen bomb was headed our way. Thousands more would head into Harlem, red eyed, with mass murder on their minds. There would suddenly be no law, no order. The whole pot that's been boiling for years could spill over and destroy us."

"And if the Mayor plays hero, then twenty thousand people could be slaughtered on Friday in the station area and all these things you've just mentioned will still happen."

"It is already one of the best kept secrets in history," Marshall said. "But if the Mayor managed to get the money and pay it to his Black Power extortionist, someone will talk—and it will all happen then."

"So there are no alternatives," Peter said. "You and Betty and I should take the next plane for the South Pole and wait there, with cotton in our ears, for it to happen."

"We may still locate the leadership," Marshall said. "We may still locate the bomb before it goes off." He looked away. "I won't be at the South Pole at five o'clock on Friday, Peter.

I've played along with the Mayor in what you call this 'brinksmanship.' If we've failed, I'll be in Grand Central Station at five o'clock on Friday. I'll face whatever I've let thousands of other people in for."

"That's what you meant when you told Marian Sims you could be dead?"

"That's what I meant."

"Does Betty know that's what you plan to do?"

"She does not, and she is not to be told." Marshall's eyes were dangerously hard. "More coffee?"

3

Peter found it difficult to assimilate the District Attorney's story. Surely the whole thing, the threat, was pure bluff. And yet there had been the bomb in the public toilet; the big bomb, the for-real bomb. He kept asking himself what would really happen if the story broke, and he had to go along with Jerry Marshall. There would be panic coupled with a kind of violence we hadn't dreamed of before now.

There was a soft knock on the study door and Betty Marshall came in without waiting for an invitation.

"I'm sorry, darling," she said. "The Mayor and Mr. Severance are here. I think you had better turn on the air conditioning."

Marshall reached out and touched his wife's hand. Physical contact seemed to be a method they had of reassuring each other. "Steamed up?" he asked.

"Boiling," Betty Marshall said.

"Charm him in, darling, if you will," Marshall said. He looked at Peter. "The Boy Wonder is going to go through

34

the roof when he finds you here. The press! Brother!"

The modern image of the politician has changed considerably over the years. The day of the cigar-chewing, derby-wearing Tammany boss is long dead. The Honorable James Ramsay, Mayor of the City of New York, was a keynoter of the new breed—comparatively young, Ivy League—Madison Avenue in style, cultivated, able to afford to serve his community because private income made his salary unimportant. The old ward-heeling pros found these new "fancy boys" surprisingly tough.

James Ramsay might have been a romantic leading man in films if he hadn't chosen politics as a career. He was tall, square jawed, level eyed, with a charming and ingratiating smile when he chose to turn it on. As he barged into Marshall's study charm was not on his mind.

"God damn it, Jerry, don't you ever dare make yourself unavailable to me! Not at a time like this. If I ever try to reach you again and you brush me off—" He stopped abruptly, his face stone hard. He had spotted Peter standing by the window. "What in God's name are you doing here, Styles?"

"Having my breakfast coffee, Mr. Mayor. Do you object?"

Ramsay made an effort. A shadow of his best smile moved his lips. "Of course not. Unfortunately we have urgent business to discuss with Jerry. Would you mind very much leaving us alone?"

"He knows the whole thing, Jim," Marshall said.

"*You've* told him?"

"Yes."

"Jesus Christ, Jerry!"

"I had to," Marshall said. "I also trust him."

35

"There's no reason on earth why—"

"Peter found Richard Sims dead on the street," Marshall said. "He called the police. He had no reason not to release the story—until I told him why he shouldn't."

"And now?" Ramsay looked straight at Peter.

"I'm willing to play along, Mr. Mayor," Peter said, "as long as I'm kept abreast of all details as they develop."

The Mayor nodded, slowly. Then he remembered the man with him; the man standing in the doorway. "You know Marty Severance, Styles?"

"We've never met," Peter said. "Hello."

"Hi," Severance said.

The Mayor had reddish-blond hair. Severance's was black. But they might have gone to the same tailor, been members of the same clubs, and probably played golf at the same handicaps.

"I kept trying to reach you, Jerry, to find out how you made out with Mrs. Sims," Ramsay said.

"Well, I think. I found Styles there. That's how it came about."

"You know the Sims, Styles?" Ramsay asked.

"No."

"Then what—?"

"I thought she'd need help. I felt guilty."

"I don't get it."

"White men killed her husband."

"Oh for God sake," Severance said. There was patronizing contempt in his voice and on his smile. "When this is all over I have one wish. Heaven deliver me from do-gooders."

"You don't like Negroes, Mr. Severance?" Peter asked.

"Negroes are about to blow our town apart," Severance said. "I'm supposed to like them? And I'm not a hypocrite,

Mr. Styles. They say they are our enemies, and I'm not Christian enough to love them in spite of it."

"How nice for you to have everything so clear," Peter said. He turned to Ramsay. "If you haven't caught up with your extortionist by noon on Friday, Mr. Mayor, will you have ten million dollars in unmarked currency ready to hand over?"

"I will *not* pay blackmail!" Ramsay said. He brought the flat of his hand down on Marshall's desk so hard the telephones jumped.

"That would be beautiful for the television cameras," Peter said. "It might even get you votes, Mr. Mayor. But not, I imagine, from the families of the people who may be blown to pieces in Grand Central on Friday night."

"I am not looking for votes!"

"I believe that," Peter said, and meant it. "But you are dealing with fanatics, Mr. Mayor. Suppose I could point a finger at Severance's telephone chum right now. You arrest him. You put him under a bright, white light, and experts try to get him to listen to reason; try to frighten him; try to bribe him with something less than ten million dollars. My guess is he'll just laugh at you. It took experts to make that bomb you found in the Commodore. Not one expert—experts. Your man on the phone is the Mouth for this scheme. But there are obviously dozens of others just as fanatical as he is."

"And you think—?"

"I'm inclined to think that anything less than ten million dollars won't change their minds," Peter said.

Ramsay lit a cigarette. His strong, capable-looking hands weren't quite steady. "You realize what capitulation means, Styles? Next week we get word that we must get up another ten million dollars or they'll blow up Lincoln Center. And the week after, they change locations and it's the United Nations building. There is no end to the possible demands, but there is an end to money with which to ransom the city."

"There's an end to what you have to take from anyone," Severance said, his white teeth gritted.

"But evidently you are going to take it two days from now, unless you can come up with something better than courageous speeches," Peter said.

"All right, you look at the alternatives," Ramsay said. "We call up the National Guard, maybe some Regular Army units. At the same moment we alert the public. The Grand Central area is evacuated and ringed with troops. No trains come in or go out. We surround Harlem with the Army to keep explosions from taking place inside or out of it. Now tell me, Styles, if you were the enemy—and let me call them the enemy for the moment without our having a discussion about black and white—if you were the enemy, what would you do?"

"Nothing," Peter said. "I would sit back, and watch, and laugh myself sick."

"Precisely," Ramsay said. "Do you have any idea what it would cost the city to call up the National Guard and the Army? Do you have any idea what it would cost the city and the city's businesses if we cut all commuter service coming in to Grand Central?"

"Hundreds of millions of dollars," Peter said.

"An hour!" Ramsay said.

"So it's much, much cheaper in money and human lives to pay the ransom. But after money will come other demands— for power, for control."

Ramsay took a deep drag on his cigarette. "Thank you for recognizing the real core of this problem, Styles. I listen to Marty who advises we move in tomorrow with the Army and wipe out the Negro community. I listen to the good people who believe so deeply in the essential goodness of man. We should get together with the rational leaders of the Negro people—men like Richard Sims, for God sake! They could, I am told, bring reason and common sense to bear on the hotheads. Well, I've talked to responsible Negroes, and they're just as much at sea as I am. Now, if you were the Mayor, Mr. Styles, what would you do?"

Peter realized that all three men in the room were waiting eagerly for his answer. They were desperate for answers.

"I think I would do two things," Peter said. "If everything else fails I would be ready to pay over ten million dollars."

"And get ready to meet the next demand?" Severance asked.

"You'd be buying time," Peter said.

"We've had three weeks' time," the Mayor said, sounding suddenly old and tired. "We've accomplished nothing."

"But the break in the case might come in the next hour, the next day," Jerry Marshall said. He didn't sound as though he believed it.

"The second thing I'd do," Peter said, "is to reconsider the risks you'd be running if this demand became public knowledge."

"You pitch for panic?" Ramsay asked.

"I don't know about the 'essential goodness' of man, Mr. Mayor," Peter said, "but I may have a deeper belief than you have in his essential courage. Mind you, I'm not suggesting that you commandeer the TV networks and press the panic button. But I would run a much greater risk of rumor starting to spread that you seem prepared to do. Your secrecy program has cut off a vital source of information from you."

"What source?"

"The working press," Peter said. "God knows it's small enough in this city now. But there are skilled reporters, and feature writers, and columnists who know this town better than you do, Mr. Mayor; better than the cop at the precinct level knows it; better than Jerry Marshall's highly competent staff knows it. They know all of it, not just specific areas. To coin a far-fetched image, they can hear a sour note in the string section just as instantly as a Toscanini. Risk the chance that there is a rotten apple in the barrel, to change metaphors. Risk the possibility that one reporter, one feature writer, may blow the secret. So one man betrays you, and ninety-nine others will announce loudly that he's full of it. If I were the mayor, Mr. Mayor, I'd run that risk and put those trained ears to the ground. It's hellishly late, but it might work."

"What could they do?" Severance asked, after a long silence.

"Let's look at it carefully," Peter said. "There can't be a whole army of plotters. Six, a dozen, two dozen. More than that and the secret would leak in their world, and believe me, there are millions of Negroes who would see the long range disaster for them. So there are only a few of them, and they must be huddling close together as the deadline gets nearer. They must be carefully rehearsing every action each one of them will take on Friday. Somewhere someone is aware that secret conclaves are being held—a landlady, a saloon keeper, a newsstand operator. Who will they talk to? Not a cop, not a city official, not an FBI man, not a soldier. They might talk to the men and women who have been their friends in the past. Somewhere someone may play a sour note and it could be heard if a trained ear was listening for it."

The Honorable James Ramsay stared at Peter as though,

somehow, the intensity of his gaze would cause Peter to disintegrate.

"It makes sense," he said, finally. "We have a little more than forty-eight hours. If somebody spills the secret, it will be almost too late for it to snowball. After noon on Friday it will be too late to matter. Will you give me a list of names?"

"Sure," Peter said. "And Jerry will add to it. He knows every good police reporter, past and present, in town. Don't forget there are a lot of good newspapermen who aren't working these days—not at the jobs they really know."

The Mayor looked at Severance. "You agree, Marty?"

Severance shrugged. "It doesn't seem there is too much to lose." . . .

The pavements were already giving off heat from the early morning sun. On a side street, as Peter headed west, he saw half a dozen little Puerto Rican children who'd got the nozzle unscrewed on a hydrant and were romping in the flow of cold water. People in the old brownstones that lined each side of the street seemed to be getting ready, calmly and efficiently, for another scorching-hot August day.

The city felt strange to Peter. It was like looking at a man, walking cheerfully along the street, unaware that he was about to die from a terminal cancer. Radios blared through open windows, blending the raucous sounds of rock-and-roll with the endlessly repeated news broadcasts, none of which carried the news which so vitally concerned the listeners. Two days away lurked violence and death.

Peter felt the need to hurry.

The sidewalk under the Hotel Molyneux's dilapidated steel awning was littered with cigarette butts, gum wrappers, and dirt.

There was a different clerk on duty at the desk. He was a young man, dark eyes set too closely together. He looked at Peter—and probably everyone else in the world—with a kind of sardonic suspicion.

"Mrs. Richard Sims, please," Peter said.

The clerk's smile was twisted. "She's all yours, dad."

"Please call her room," Peter said, gesturing toward the house phone, "and tell her Mr. Styles would like to see her."

"You can go up, dad. Her husband's out."

"Call," Peter said, sharply.

"This ain't the Waldorf, dad," the clerk said. "You want to mess around with that kind of dame, go ahead and mess. Room 402."

Peter reached quickly across the desk, caught the clerk by the front of his coat, and yanked him close. He hit him a stinging slap across the mouth. As he did it he wondered what the hell had gotten into him. All the rage that had been boiling in him since the moment he'd seen Sims laying on the pavement in Irving Place had suddenly exploded against this miserable jerk.

"Call!" Peter said.

The clerk's face had turned parchment white. A little trickle of blood ran down from the corner of his mouth. He picked up the phone and plugged in a connection on the ancient switchboard.

"Someone named Styles wants to see you," he said, in a sullen voice. He put down the phone. "So go up," he said to Peter, blotting at the corner of his mouth with the back of his hand.

Peter turned toward the old self-service elevator, shaken by his own violence. Halfway to the elevator the clerk's voice reached him.

"I won't forget, dad," the clerk said.

Peter ignored him. The elevator creaked its way to the fourth floor. Marian Sims stood in the open doorway to 402.

"You have some news?" she asked, as he reached her.

"Not about your husband, Mrs. Sims," Peter said. "But I need to talk to you."

"Please come in."

He followed her into the book-lined room. "I'd just made myself some coffee," the girl said.

"I've been drinking coffee ever since I left here," Peter said. "But—yes. Black, if I may."

She busied herself for a moment at the little two burner gas stove on a shelf in the corner. Peter found himself making a re-assessment of her. Her face was handsome, not pretty. The bone structure was good—high cheekbones, a firm chin, a straight, firm mouth. Her eyes, still showing a hint of tears that must have come in torrents when she was alone, were china blue. There were little reflections of red in the blond hair. Seen across any crowded room he'd have written her down as someone with a degree of cultivation, and certainly with character.

She had changed from the housecoat she'd worn earlier into a grey flannel skirt, stylishly short, and a pink cardigan, the sleeves rolled up to her elbows. She was a type, he thought, he'd seen at Vassar, or Smith, or Bryn Mawr.

"You must have some kind of magic," she said, as she brought the coffee. "You're the first guest who's ever been announced from downstairs. How did you manage?"

"I clouted him one across the mouth," Peter said.

"Well," she said, bitterly, "I'd planned to move anyway."

43

"What do you mean 'anyway'?"

"The clerk is the owner's son," she said. "We don't have a lease here. You don't give a mixed couple like us a lease. You had something on your mind, Mr. Styles?"

He nodded. "I'm going to take the chance of filling you in on the rest of Jerry Marshall's problem—the reason he wants to bury the story of your husband's death for forty-eight hours."

"I think it would help me to bear the whole situation if I knew," she said.

He told her, quickly, concisely—the man on the phone, the demand for money or else, the bomb in the station, the running out of time. She listened, her eyes widening. When he had finished she lit a cigarette, like someone not really accustomed to smoking.

"We've heard this kind of talk—oh, for a year," she said. "Forget riots—aim at specific targets."

"Richard was against it?"

"There is a thing called backlash," she said. "Put two fighters together in a ring and the best fighter will win. Put two mobs together and the one with the most numbers will win—sheer weight of bodies. The cause won't matter. The skill of any one fighter won't matter. Numbers count—and we are outnumbered."

She said "we" meaning Negroes. His eyes narrowed.

"You're like most nice, decent liberal people," she said. "Reason tells you that I'm perfectly justified to have been married to Richard. But you can't help being slightly revolted by the idea. I'm like a leper with a tinkling bell around my neck. 'Unclean! Unclean!' "

"I haven't really had time to think about it, Marian, or to know how I feel."

"Thank you, Peter. Thank you for not protesting loudly

44

and nobly that you have no feeling about it." She drew a deep breath. "You came here because you want me to do something for you, and you've made it quite clear there's no time for philosophical chit-chat."

"There is a Negro newspaperman named Nathan Jones," Peter said. "I know that he's a friend of your husband's because I remember he wrote a foreword to one of Richard's books of poems. I want to get to him—not as Peter Styles, writer, but as Peter Styles, friend of yours."

"You're going to tell him what you've told me?"

"Someone on the Negro side has got to work for us, listen for us, use his influence for us."

Marian's laugh had an edge to it. "You expect Nate Jones to work for you? Peter, how naive can you be? Nate hates your guts—all white guts. He hates you so much he could even be a part of this conspiracy you're fighting."

"But he's a reasonable man."

"Within his own frame of reference, Peter."

"A reasonable man will understand how devastating the backlash will be, if this scheme is carried out on Friday."

"I'll have to lie to him," Marian said, staring past Peter and the blank window.

"Lie?"

"He wouldn't do me a favor, Peter. He thinks that I, simply by existing, have weakened Richard's effectiveness as a fighter for the cause. I will have to tell him—" and Marian's voice was suddenly unsteady—"tell him that Richard wants him to talk to you. He might do it for Richard."

"Please," Peter said. "There's no time to deal with in-betweens. Nathan Jones is at the top of some heap. I need to get to him."

Marian went over to what had been Richard's work table.

45

From a center drawer she took a small address book, found a number, and dialed it on the telephone.

"Nathan? Marian Sims here . . . Well; thank you." Her eyes contracted. "Yes, he's fine. I'm calling you for him. He wants you to see a man . . . Peter Styles . . . Yes, he's the columnist for *Newsview* . . . Please, Nathan. You know Richard wouldn't send him to you to do some fancy liberal piece. . . . I think you'll have to let Mr. Styles tell you what he wants . . . Yes, he's here now. . . . Nathan, does it have to be there? . . . Very well, I'll tell him." Marian put down the phone. "There's a bar and grill at One hundred twenty-seventh Street and Lenox Avenue, Peter. Nathan will be there in half an hour and he'll wait ten minutes for you."

"Thank you."

"Could you keep in touch?" she asked. "Let me know how—how it goes?"

"I'll keep in touch," Peter said . . .

Peter took a taxi north into Harlem. At One hundred twenty-fifth Street the taxi pulled over to the curb.

Peter leaned forward. "It's two blocks north of here," he said to the driver.

"Sorry, Mac, this is as far as I go," the driver said.

"What's wrong?"

"You been noticing down the side streets as we came north?" the driver asked. The name on his license card was David Schneider. "No kids. Hot day like this people are usually starting to drape themselves out on the fire escapes. Whole place is too goddam quiet. If I was you, Mac, unless my business was real important, I'd head back downtown."

"My business is real important," Peter said.

"I was up here before the trouble a year ago," Schneider

46

said. "It was like this. The people knew. They had their kids in off the streets. You notice half the little stores ain't opened up this morning?"

One hundred twenty-fifth Street was one of the busiest crosstown arteries in the city. It looked, Peter saw, like a Sunday. Schneider was right. Many stores hadn't opened. Buses seemed to carry relatively few passengers. He paid the driver and got out. Sweat was running down inside his shirt. It was hot, hot, hot—and curiously still.

"Have fun," Schneider said, and whipped his cab around in a forbidden U-turn and streaked away downtown.

Peter started north, walking briskly. He had the unpleasant feeling that he was being watched from behind curtained windows. The people he passed on the street, all Negro, eyed him with suspicion. There was, certainly, something in the air.

At One hundred twenty-seventh Street he saw the bar and grill sign. A tall Negro man was standing outside the entrance. He seemed to be watching for someone. When he saw Peter, he turned and went quickly into the place.

Peter paused for a moment to wipe his face with a white linen handkerchief. Then he went in.

The heat was oppressive. There was no air conditioning. A long bar ran from one end of the place to the other, facing a row of booths. A bartender stood wiping glasses, watching Peter as he came in. Three men stood at the bar, one of them the tall man Peter had seen out on the sidewalk a moment ago. In the farthest booth, at the end of the place, a man sat, drumming on the table with strong square fingers. His head was shaven close. He had a thin black mustache and a small goatee. He was wearing black glasses, black as his skin. A long, thin cigar burned in an ash tray in front of him.

47

Peter walked down the length of the room. "Nathan Jones?" he asked.

"Nathan Hale Jones," the man said. He had a controlled, actor's voice—quiet, yet so projected that the other men at the far end of the bar could obviously hear him without difficulty. "You're late, Mr. Styles."

Peter glanced at his watch. "Twenty-six minutes," he said. "You gave me forty."

"About ten years late, Mr. Styles," Jones said. "Sit down if you want."

Peter sat. He heard a sound that made him turn. The bartender had moved out to the entrance door. He had thrown two heavy iron bolts. There would be no more customers for a while.

"My office," Jones said, drily. He picked up the cigar and tapped grey ash into the glass tray. "How is Marian taking it?"

Peter felt a little crawling sensation along his spine. "Taking what?"

"Richard's murder," Jones said, casually. He smiled. It was mildly contemptuous. "The attempts at secrecy have been rather childish, Styles. How did you persuade Marian to sit on it?"

"How did you know about it?" Peter asked.

"The world is full of cowards," Jones said. "A man who lives on Irving Place—a black man. He saw it all. He watched, sweating I suppose, teeth chattering I suppose. Then he screwed up the enormous courage to call someone up here —miles away. Far too late to be any use to Richard."

"Can he identify the men?"

"It was dark," Jones said. He tasted his cigar. "They were white—nine feet tall. Our brave friend couldn't be persuaded

48

to go out on the street, but he watched. He saw you arrive, he saw you go. By then, we had a friend or two watching. We know you went to Marian. We know that great humanitarian, Jerome Marshall, arrived on the scene with one of his police dogs. We know that when you left, Marian made no attempt to communicate with any of Richard's friends."

"And that is why the quiet up here?" Peter asked.

A shaft of sunlight hit Jones' black glasses and they glittered. "We're getting ready for Friday," he said quietly. "That's what you wanted to talk to me about, wasn't it?"

Peter heard his breath exhale in a kind of shuddering sigh. "Thanks for not beating around the bush," he said.

"You won't like it," Jones said.

"I like the fact that we can talk about it. There is so little time."

"The city is going to pay?" Jones asked.

"Pay on Friday? Pay the following Friday? Pay the Friday after that—and forever?"

"It would gain time," Jones said.

Peter reached in his pocket for his pipe. "I think you will choose not to believe what I tell you," he said. "Of course they don't want the threatened disaster. But more than that, they fear the aftermath; not only here but all over the country. There will be no controlling the backlash, both legal and illegal."

Jones looked at his cigar. It had gone out. Peter flicked on his lighter and held it.

"You don't have to be that integrated, White Man," Jones said.

"Come on, cut that out!" Peter said, sharply.

Jones smiled. He allowed Peter to hold the lighter until his

49

cigar was going. "You fear the backlash?" he said. "We've lived with backlash all our lives. I sit here, Styles, and I think of being torn to pieces by a mob, after Friday, and I think, 'Why not? If not Friday then sooner or later.' Maybe it would be a good thing. Maybe it would so shatter the consciences of the people, when the bloody job was done, that there would be some real thought about the black man's place in this world. You fear the atom bomb, Styles, but it might be better if it was dropped, all over hell. Maybe there would then be six people left who'd try to start up some kind of a decent world."

"Can the Friday business be stopped?"

"By paying ten million dollars," Jones said.

"Are you a part of it?"

Jones laughed. "Would I tell you, White Man? It has been a habit of my misbegotten people to name their children after great heroes. After the Civil War they were mostly named 'Lincoln.' Today the woods are full of young black men named 'Roosevelt.' In sports—all over. My family chose to name me 'Nathan Hale.' One life to give for my country. I prefer to give up that life fighting you in the streets, White Man, than languishing in one of your antiquated jails."

"You want all the people in all the Negro ghettos in this country wiped out, just so you can enjoy the luxury of manning the barricades?"

A look of pain twisted the black face. Peter wished he could see the eyes behind the impenetrable glasses.

"Believe it or not," Jones said, "I am not a party to the conspiracy. Believe it or not I have been working night and day to discover who is back of it."

"How did you come to hear of it?"

"We have ears, man," Jones said. "Black ears and white ears—in high places."

50

"And you would stop it if you could?"

Jones looked past Peter into space. "I would reason," he said. "What could be done with that ten million dollars? It might build a dozen new tenements, with heat and hot water, and maybe a garbage disposal unit. We need a thousand of them. But I would like to believe that, somehow, the money would be used for our people. Maybe a clinic. Maybe a better school or two."

"And you doubt it will be used for your people?"

"I believe the motive is desperate rage," Jones said, quietly. "I believe it is a thirst for power. Our turn to pipe the tune. A tit-for-tat motive. No one will benefit from it. Everyone will be hurt. A few fanatics will be temporarily rich if the city pays."

"So you are willing to help?"

"I wish I knew how," Jones said. "You understand, I don't want to help you. I want to help my own people." He shook his head, slowly. "It is something new, White Man. We are not a close-mouthed people. This threat has been in the wind for almost a month. Would you believe that no one has gotten a little drunk and talked a little too much? Would you believe I haven't seen an extra swagger, a secret smirk? Would you believe that no woman, afraid for the lives of her children, has reported any wild talk from her man? I have told you that I have ears that listen in the highest places, in the secret conclaves of the Mayor himself. I would have said that nothing here in Harlem could be a secret I couldn't probe. This secret is buried in a tomb I can't even locate." He drew a deep breath. "You can buy this as the truth, or you can consider me a cynical liar and a party to the conspiracy."

"Did Richard Sims know what was going on?" Peter asked.

"Not from me. You see, alas man, Richard couldn't be

trusted. He had joined up with the enemy."

"Marian?"

Jones nodded.

"She thinks of herself as Negro. She thinks of Richard's cause as her cause."

"A nice little girl from Vassar College," Jones said. "They teach 'em there not to be bigoted, you understand, man? The color of a man's skin, they teach 'em, makes no difference. Black ideas are as good as white ideas. And if a 'nigger' asks you to dance at the Senior Prom, you dance, you don't flinch. Get it? And when the dance is over, the other unbigoted little white girls crowd around and ask, 'Could you tell, dancing with him, that Negroes are built sexually bigger than white men?' So a brilliant young Negro poet went to Vassar to read his verse to the literary group. Afterwards one of the unbigoted students, our Maid Marian, invited the poet to have a hamburger and coffee with her, right out in public. So Richard accepted the invitation and he turned on his special magic, which was gentle, and kind, and full of dreams— dreams that the color of his skin really didn't matter. And I can only guess the girl went home afterwards and hung onto herself in bed, not sleeping, and telling herself over and over that it didn't really matter what color his skin was. And she was so full of liberal ideas, and so determined not to be bigoted, and so bent on being a heroine that when Richard, full of his own dreams, made a pass at her she gritted her teeth and said 'yes.' And then, I daresay to her enormous surprise, she found out it was so. It didn't matter. He was a kind, gentle, sensitive man. But, of course, it did matter. His people and her people all began to hate. And they lived in that crumb-joint and they had only each other. Richard tried to go on servicing and educating his people, but he wasn't one of

52

them anymore. He was a white lover. And so he died, not because he knew a secret someone was afraid he'd tell. I think he died—and I'm only guessing—because he'd defiled a white woman who happened to love him."

"You don't think there is any connection between his murder and the plan for Friday?"

"I told you, man, I'm guessing."

"So what do you advise as a course of action?"

Jones shrugged. "I, for one, keep listening and looking. If I hear nothing, and the Mayor doesn't pay up on time, I'll sit here listening, and I'll hear the bomb go off, and I'll walk out into the street and wait for the first avenging white man with a hot gun in his hand—and I'll hope to kill him and a few others before they tramp me to death."

"And I—what do I do?" Peter asked.

"Try to persuade the Mayor to pay—to give us time," Jones said.

"And if I fail?"

"Leave town, man, on the first plane out. And take anyone you really care about with you. You got a scarlet letter on your chest, man. You're marked—with a great big A."

"An A?"

"Animal lover," Jones said. "You acted as a friend to a nigger."

Peter dropped his unlighted pipe back into his pocket. "Make a deal?" he asked.

"I doubt it."

"If you hear anything will you tell me? And if I hear anything I'll tell you."

"I promise you nothing, man. It's a black problem, and if it can be handled at all it will be handled without help from the enemy."

"How can I reach you?" Peter asked. "Because I wasn't making a trade. If I hear anything that could be helpful, I'll pass it on to you."

Jones smiled, mirthlessly. "By God, I believe you would." He took a pencil out of his pocket and scribbled a number on a paper napkin. "Call this number. You won't get me, but say where I can get you."

Peter stood up. He heard the bartender slide open the bolts on the door.

"One suggestion," Jones said.

"Yes?"

"Persuade Marian to leave town till things are cooled. The whites may want her for whoring around with a big, black buck. And the blacks may want her for contaminating a good man. She can't go to her family. Maybe you got a friend, man—some other unbigoted Vassar girl who might take her in?"

"I'll talk to her," Peter said . . .

Somehow the heat seemed even more intense as Peter stepped out on to Lenox Avenue. The sun was rising high in the sky and Peter realized that it must be approaching the noon hour. He checked on his watch. Four minutes to twelve; almost exactly forty-eight hours to the moment of decision for the Honorable James Ramsay. To pay or not to pay.

No taxi cruised the curiously deserted streets of Harlem. Peter headed toward the nearest subway station. He was instinctively conscious that he was being followed. He turned, and saw the tall black sentry who had been waiting for him to arrive at the bar and grill. He was clearly one of Nathan Jones' men. Jones had made no effort to keep their conversation unheard. Peter wondered, uneasily, whether the tall man was there to spy or to protect.

He ducked down into the subway, bought himself a token, and went out onto the platform. Noon on a Wednesday, and the platform was deserted. It was so deserted that he could hear footsteps on the stairway from the street. The tall man was there. He made no move to pay his way through the turnstile; he just stood by the change booth watching Peter. Evidently Nathan Hale Jones wanted to be sure that Peter got out of 'his country' without being molested.

The steaming hot subway car with its sleepy-looking passengers was a relief. Peter stood near the center doors, rolling slightly with the swaying cars. It had been his intention to go all the way downtown to his apartment. He badly wanted a change of clothes. He also wanted to talk privately with Frank Devery, his managing editor at *Newsview*. There were one or two members of the magazine's staff whose talents he felt he could use for the next few days. But on impulse, he got off at the Eighty-sixth Street stop on the East Side and took a taxi across the Park to the Hotel Molyneaux. Nathan Jones' final advice to persuade Marian to leave town had preyed on him. Better talk to her now than wait till he was up to his neck in the last tense hours of searching for the men who threatened the lives of God alone knew how many thousands of innocent people.

In the bright noon sunshine, the Molyneaux looked even dingier than it had at dawn. Peter went into the lobby. His young friend with the close set eyes was still on duty at the desk. He didn't trust his temper so he decided to skip the courtesy of warning Marian that he was on his way up.

He stepped into the elevator. Someone had just mopped

the floor of the car and it was still damp. The car creaked its way to the fourth floor and Peter got out and walked along to the door of 402. He raised his hand to knock, and then hesitated. The wood around the lock of the door was freshly splintered. He could have sworn it hadn't been that way an hour and a half ago. He gave the door a tentative little push with his fingertips and it swung slowly inward.

"Marian!" he called out, sharply.

The room was a shambles. Furniture had been tipped over, the neat covers on the overstuffed chairs and the couch ripped and torn. Richard's typewriter had been hurled into a corner, and lay there, a crumpled piece of junk. Nearly all the books had been wrenched out of the bookcases and someone had taken the time to tear many of them loose from their bindings. The telephone had been ripped from its wall connection.

"Marian!"

There was only the bathroom where she could be, and that door stood open. He looked in. She wasn't there.

He walked around behind the desk. He remembered seeing her put the card Lieutenant Pike had given her in the center drawer—the card with the number on it that would bring her help.

The card was there but the phone was useless.

PART TWO

1

Peter didn't wait for the elevator. He ran down the four short flights of stairs to the lobby. He could have sworn the leering clerk with the close set eyes was waiting for him.

Peter put Pike's card down on the desk.

"Be good enough to call this number," he said.

The clerk had backed away out of arm's reach. His smile was insolent. "There's a pay phone in the drugstore next door," he said.

Peter braced himself on his one good leg and swung himself up so that he was sitting on the desk. He twisted around and came down on the other side next to the clerk. He plugged in the switchboard and dialed a number. After a moment a man's voice answered.

"Yes, Mrs. Sims?"

"It's not Mrs. Sims," Peter said. "Styles here. I've just been up to Mrs. Sims' room. The place has been wrecked and she isn't there."

"On our way," the man said, and the phone clicked off.

Peter turned to the clerk, who'd lost his smile. "Now, buster, let's you and I stop playing games. Sombody smashed open the door of 402. They've wrecked the place, smashed furniture, thrown a typewriter around, and gone off with Mrs. Sims. This couldn't have happened without a considerable amount of noise."

"It's four floors up." The clerk had lost all vestiges of jauntiness. "I couldn't hear anything down here."

"But other people on that floor could. No complaints?"

"There's nobody on Four during the day. All working people."

"Something wrong, Georgie?" a husky voice asked behind Peter.

The voice belonged to a grossly fat man, shirtsleeved, a frayed cigar in one corner of his mouth. Behind him was a heavy set man in blue coveralls.

"This punk is trying to strong arm me," the clerk blubbered.

"Okay, Georgie, we'll just strong arm him out of there," the fat man said. "Irving!"

The man in the coveralls came forward. His muscles bulged.

"Like thirty seconds to get out of there, fellow," the fat man said to Peter. His smile reminded Peter of the clerk's. Father and son, Marian had said. "Are you the manager here?" he asked.

"I am the owner," the fat man said. "Paul Savage. I know you from somewhere, don't I?"

"His name is Styles," Georgie said. "He's the one I told you about that clouted me a while back."

"Maybe you'd ought to be taught some manners," the fat man said. "Your thirty seconds is up. Irving!"

Two men came through the revolving door from the street

58

just as Irving hoisted himself up onto the desk and reached for Peter.

"Hold it, Irving," the fat man said. "I smell fuzz."

The two men came to the desk. "Mr. Styles?" the first one said. "Sergeant McComas."

"I had a little trouble trying to use the phone," Peter said. "This man is the manager, the clerk is his son, and superman's name is Irving. Georgie, the clerk, claims he heard nothing, saw nothing."

"What's supposed to be wrong?" the fat man asked.

"Somebody broke into Mrs. Sims' room, ripped the place apart, and took Mrs. Sims away with them," Peter said.

"Oh her," the fat man said.

"Let's go up and have a look," McComas said. "All of us."

"Georgie can't leave the desk," the fat man said.

"Georgie will leave the desk," McComas said.

Peter swung his way over the top of the desk. McComas introduced his partner, Detective Halligan.

"Pike is going to raise hell if anything has happened to her," Halligan said.

"Something has happened to her," Peter said.

"We were stationed across the street," McComas said. "She certainly didn't go out the front door here. We've had it under surveillance since we took over about six this morning. Saw you come and go the first time, and come back a few minutes ago. We haven't seen anyone come or go who concerned us any."

They went upstairs, herding the owner, Georgie and Irving ahead of them.

"Sweet Sue!" McComas said, when he opened the door of 402.

"Georgie would like us to believe that nobody heard what

59

was going on here," Peter said. "A cyclone hit this place. Nothing quiet about it."

McComas looked at Georgie.

"I'm Paul Savage, like I told Mr. Styles, the owner," the fat man said. "Georgie here is my son. Irving is the engineer and custodian."

"Check the adjoining rooms," McComas said to Halligan, as though the fat man hadn't spoken.

"I take it she didn't call you?" Peter said.

McComas shook his head. He looked down at the splintered doorjamb and the broken lock. "Flimsy to start with," he said. "Someone like Irving here—come open with one good shoulder block, wouldn't it, Irving?"

"I suppose it would," Irving said.

"She never had a chance to call," McComas said. "Whoever it was just exploded in. Hook up that telephone, Irving."

"You got to have a telephone man for that," Irving said.

"I see a screw driver there in your pocket. That's all you need."

"According to the union—"

McComas, who was a good six inches shorter and forty pounds lighter than Irving did the unexpected. He gave the big man a brutal kick in the shins that doubled him over, swearing in pain.

"Whenever I muff a job I always take it out on someone completely innocent of any blame," McComas said. "Now hook up that phone, Irving."

"Police brutality!" Georgie shrieked.

"You like a sample?" McComas asked, very polite.

"Now, now, Sergeant. Take it easy," the fat man said. His

eyes were amber slits of anger, but his voice was soothing.

"All I want is cooperation," McComas said. "You be a witness, Mr. Styles. All I asked for was cooperation. He don't need a lawyer for that, does he?"

Peter wasn't listening. A kind of sick feeling had come over him as he looked around the room. It was the symptom of a disease. You could smell violence for the sheer joy of it. You could smell hate. How much courage can one human being be expected to show? It had taken courage for Marian Sims to live at all, having made the decision she had made about her marriage. Then, like lefts and rights from a heavyweight fighter, the murder of her husband; the complete and total loneliness resulting from the best of two worlds turning their backs on her; and then the blood-curdling sound of her door smashing in; man or men caught up in a maniacal fury, destroying everything that had been precious to Richard—his books, his writing tools. And his wife?

"No one appears to be in the rooms along the hall." Halligan had come back. "Fire stair at the end of the hall." Cold grey eyes fixed on the fat man. "Looks more like a garbage chute than a way out. About a thousand violations of the fire laws, I'd say. It's hard to tell whether anyone used it as a way out. Trash has been walked over for months."

"She went or was taken somewhere," McComas said. He turned to Georgie. "You been on the desk all morning—say since Mr. Styles was here the first time?"

"Yeah, sure," Georgie said.

"You didn't hear anything? You didn't see anyone come in the lobby and go up stairs?"

"No one I didn't know had a right to—except Mr. Styles."

"He had a right," McComas said.

"More important," Halligan said. "You didn't see anyone leave with Mrs. Sims in tow?"

"I sure didn't."

"The elevator floor had just been mopped," Peter heard himself say.

"That elevator go down into the basement, Irving?" McComas asked the custodian.

"Sure."

"That's your hangout, isn't it, Irving? Anybody go out that way—with Mrs. Sims?"

"I didn't see anybody use the basement."

"You mop the floor of the cage?"

"Sure. Routine."

"Like probably once a year," Halligan said.

"You thought there might have been blood, Mr. Styles?"

"I wondered," Peter said.

"I've had about enough of this," the fat man said, not doing a very good job of concealing his anger. "I run a decent place here. I—"

"You run a combination whorehouse, flophouse, and hideout for petty crooks," Halligan said. "Let's face it."

"Prove it, friend!" the fat man said.

"After we find Mrs. Sims, I may just take time out to do that," Halligan said. "And unless we get a little better cooperation from you, Savage, we may take the whole goddam place apart, brick by brick, looking for her."

"Look, if I knew where she was or what happened to her I'd tell you," Savage said. "I tried to be nice to the Simses, didn't I? I let them live here, didn't I—a black man and a white woman? I didn't ask to see their marriage license, did I? I took their word they were married. I let 'em stay here even though the other guests didn't like it—a black man and a white woman."

"That phone working yet, Irving?" McComas asked.

The custodian had re-attached the phone line to the little square metal box on the baseboard. "It's okay," he said. . . .

Lieutenant Pike's men almost literally carried out Halligan's threat to take the Molyneaux apart brick by brick. Fingerprint men and photographers went over every square inch of the wrecked room, the elevator, the fire stairs, the basement. The police lab reported that, in spite of the mopping, there were traces of human blood on the linoleum floor of the elevator. The fat man and Georgie and Irving and a half dozen other employees of the grimy hotel were being questioned and re-questioned, hour after hour, without results. People in the neighborhood had seen nothing to attract particular attention.

Lieutenant Pike and Jerry Marshall, the District Attorney, had come onto the scene at the Molyneaux. These were two old pros at the business of murder, and Peter, watching them, had the feeling that they'd taken up the challenge of Richard Sims' murder and Marian's disappearance with something like eagerness. From time to time, Peter saw Jerry Marshall look at his watch. Time was slipping by. Forty-five hours to the blackmail deadline. Marshall knew he should be combing the city for the men who were threatening thousands of lives. But that was so damned intangible. They didn't have a single lead, except the mocking telephone voice that talked to Severance. Murder was something real; something Pike and Marshall knew how to get their teeth into; their dish, their profession, their lives.

Peter had gone over his part of the story several times with Marshall, including his visit to Harlem and his talk with

Nathan Jones. They had gone down to a little coffee shop next door to the hotel while the Homicide technicians continued to go over Marian's room with their little vacuum cleaners, their cameras, their dusting powders.

"What can they hope to find?" Peter asked, aware that he was close to physical exhaustion. It was just twelve hours since Timmy Fallon had waked him with the story of Richard Sims' beating and death.

"Those sonsofbitches in the hotel are lying in their teeth," Marshall said. "They have to know how she was taken out. Not through the lobby. McComas and Halligan would have seen her if she'd been brought out the front door. It had to be through the basement. Someone had to tell Irving to mop up the blood in the elevator car. In the old days we'd have beaten the bewadding out of them until they told us. Now somebody in a judge's hat will turn up and tell us to play it cool. McComas is probably already in trouble for kicking that big baboon in the shins." Marshall brought his fist down on the table. His ordinarily mild grey eyes were cold as two newly-minted dimes. "Time is the thing, God damn it! It's been a good two hours since she was taken—more if it happened immediately after you left her to go to Harlem. She can be well out of my jurisdiction. If they have access to a plane, she could be half way to Mexico."

"If she's alive," Peter said, staring at his cooling coffee.

"I promised her she'd be safe and I let her down," Marshall said. "Oh, we'll get on the trail. That's our business. She's not in the hotel, that's for certain. We've covered every inch of it. There's no place to hide a prisoner—or a body. Someone came in from the outside and took her away. Those foolish-looking guys collecting dust will come up with something; dirt on the rugs or in the basement that doesn't belong in the

64

hotel; dirt we may be able to trace to somewhere else. We place them somewhere else that way, and perhaps come up with a witness we haven't dreamed of yet. But it will take time; days maybe. And after Friday it won't matter. We may all be dead by then." He looked at his watch. "You and I are supposed to be meeting with the masterminds at four o'clock. My apartment."

"The Mayor?"

"And Severance, and the Governor perhaps, and a couple of generals in case they call out the National Guard and the Army, and Inspector Mayberry of the Bomb Squad, and a few more newsmen like you, let in on the secret at your suggestion."

"You don't think that was a good idea?"

"What has it got you so far, Peter? It took you two hours to get a lot of double talk out of Nathan Jones. We haven't got time for failures!" Marshall pressed his finger tips against his closed eyes. "I'm sorry, Peter," he said. "It's not your fault. I'm worn a little thin, I guess."

"Do you see any connection between what's happened to Richard and Marian Sims and the main problem?" Peter asked.

"Oh, there's a connection," Marshall said. "We're sitting on the edge of a holocaust, a war between black and white. What's happened to the Simses is a symptom of it, a warning of how hot the climate is. Direct connection? Who knows?"

McComas came in from the street and spotted them at their corner table.

"Sorry, but so far zero, Mr. Marshall," he said when he joined them. "Take the lab hours to analyze what the boys have picked up in their vacuums. Nothing in the cellar. Not another drop of blood. Nothing."

"Take them all downtown," Marshall said. "Fatso, the boy, Irving. Book 'em as accessories to a homicide. Some smart lawyer will spring 'em before supper time, but let's keep on their backs. Constant surveillance. We want to know who they talk to on the telephone, who they see, how they act."

"Right." McComas hesitated. "One thing. There was a little money in the apartment; about a hundred and sixty bucks in a wallet in a bureau drawer. Some modest little pieces of jewelry. There were address books with phone numbers, stuff like that. Nothing touched. Someone just wrecked the joint because they hated her—and him."

"That is not news, friend," Marshall said.

"Just for the record," McComas said. "That smart lawyer might try to call it an ordinary robbery. It wasn't."

"I had a dream," Marshall said. "I dreamed that Sims was killed because he had information about the main show, and his wife silenced on the chance she might know too. But if there were any names, or phone numbers, or documents that would help us, they'd be gone and we'd have no way of knowing."

"And the wreckage to make us think they *weren't* looking for anything," McComas said. "Just what we are thinking."

Marshall nodded. "But how does the song go? 'Wishing Won't Make It So'?"

"I wondered about Marian's family," Peter said.

"People named Harding," McComas said. "Live up in Connecticut somewhere—place called Lakeview. I had your office call them, Mr. Marshall."

"They're coming?"

"According to Joe Samuels, who called, they just said 'Thank you.'"

"Family will spread the word," Marshall said, frowning.

"They were warned," McComas said. "Secrecy might be essential to getting her back."

"According to Marian she was already dead as far as they are concerned," Peter said.

2

The large living room in Jerome Marshall's apartment was cool, thanks to an efficient air-conditioning system. Venetian blinds shut out the hot sun that beat down on the park across the way. It was just after four in the afternoon.

Betty Marshall had set up an efficient-looking bar on a stretcher table at the west end of the room. There were bowls of potato chips and mixed nuts and cheese crackers. Betty herself had evaporated into the far reaches somewhere.

Peter and Jerry Marshall arrived together, and almost immediately others began to come. First there was a big, broad-shouldered man with a dour face who turned out to be Inspector Mayberry of the Bomb Squad. He was followed almost immediately by two military men, Lieutenant General Danvers of the Army and General Franklin of the National Guard.

Peter was introduced and stood off in a corner. Marshall was acting as host. The men talked very quietly, as if they were in church. Then came two newsmen whom Peter knew and waved to, Al Jaquith of the Associated Press and George

Bauersmith who represented the news bureau at one of the major television networks. Police Commissioner O'Connor arrived and huddled with Marshall.

The bigwigs were last—the Honorable James Ramsay, with Martin Severance and the Governor of the State, the Honorable Hugh Whelan. There was no fanfare of trumpets, but they came into the room on a high key, smiling, hearty. A couple of young men, evidently on the Governor's staff, remained in the background.

Drinks were poured. Chairs were pulled up in a rough circle. Peter stood in his corner, ignoring the chair that was placed for him.

"Well, gentlemen," Ramsay said, "here we are. Time marches on inexorably. We are now a little less than forty-four hours away from the deadline of noon on Friday. I take it, Jerry, there is no new development or I'd have heard from you. No breakthrough of any kind?"

"Nothing," Marshall said. "The Police Commissioner and I have nothing new to offer." He hesitated. "You all know of the murder of Richard Sims last night. We've kept it buried in case it might trigger things ahead of time. A little past noon today, Mrs. Sims was abducted from her room at the Hotel Molyneaux, just a few blocks from here. The place was wrecked. But we have no real reason to assume there is any connection between these two things and the main event."

"There are no leads in either case?" the Governor asked.

"We're working on them, sir," O'Connor said.

"Well, gentlemen, we have to make decisions and we have to make them now," Ramsay said. "If we are even to consider meeting the blackmailer's demands, paying the money, we have to move at once. The task of raising that much currency in untraceable bills of small denominations is not simple; it can't be put off till the last minute."

"You're not seriously considering paying?" General Danvers, the army man, asked.

"I think we have to be prepared for it as a last minute eventuality, General," Ramsay said.

"It's unthinkable. It's unthinkable that you'll knuckle under," Danvers said.

Ramsay's professional placating smile was weary. "I've lived with this for more than three weeks, General. I've gone round and round with it until I'm dizzy. I've been exhausted by my own anger. I've been sick with fear of what may happen to the city and its people. In the privacy of my own bathroom, General, looking at myself in the mirror, I've played it tough, I've played it reasonably, and I've played it like a coward. I have come to the point now where I am convinced of one thing. We must be ready to pay, if we decide that we must at the last minute."

"Which will leave us in the position with being presented with the same situation all over again in a week, a month," Martin Severance said.

"If we don't pay and we can't stop it," Ramsay said, "God knows how many thousands of people will die. I don't think I could live with the knowledge on my conscience that I hadn't been prepared to change my mind at the last minute. I have taken steps to make arrangements to raise the money in cash. That doesn't mean I'm committed to paying it, gentlemen. It does mean that I haven't closed the door on our only out."

"I'd like to put a question before this meeting," General Franklin of the National Guard said.

"By all means, General."

70

"You have kept this whole thing a secret from the public and, as I understand it, until today from the press." He glanced at Peter and the two other newsmen. "Your reason for this was that you feared a white backlash of such proportions that the city would become a seething hotbed of riots and violence."

"Not only here," the Governor said quietly, "but in cities all over the nation. Perhaps a full scale destruction of a whole segment of our population, the end of any kind of civil rights, of true democracy. Bloodshed beyond belief, General, with world opinion, quite justifiably, labeling us as monsters."

"Screw world opinion," General Danvers said. "World opinion is something that's turned on and off at will by the Communists. I don't give a damn for world opinion."

"I'd like to keep this discussion where it belongs," the Mayor said. "A city problem, my problem, that has to be solved in the next forty-three hours. I'd like to ask you a question, Inspector Mayberry."

"Yes, sir," the Bomb Squad expert said.

"Suppose we were to shut off Grand Central Station tonight, after the rush hour. No more incoming trains. All rolling stock in the station moved out into the suburban yards. Suppose we shut off all the surrounding streets and avenues. Suppose we removed all personnel from the station, Inspector, and turned it over to you—and the National Guard. Suppose we did all that, could you keep the bomb from being brought into the station?"

"If it isn't already there," Mayberry said. "Ninety-five percent certain."

"The other five percent?"

Mayberry gave the National Guard General, Franklin, a wry smile. "I can't vouch for every man in the General's army," he said.

"And your own men?" Franklin asked, angrily.

"Ninety-five percent certain," Mayberry said.

"But we would save the lives of the thousands of commuters who would normally be in the station on Friday night, even if the bomb got by you, Inspector."

"You would save some people. Not the real estate," Mayberry said.

"Is there any reason to believe the bomb is there now?" the Governor asked.

"We are dealing with fanatics," Mayberry said, "but very shrewd fanatics. It has been my theory that the bomb isn't there. We've been watching and spot-checking for two weeks. We know the threat isn't hot air. If they can produce a duplicate of the bomb they let us find in the men's room at the Commodore, they can do what they threaten. There's no reason to assume they can't duplicate it. It wouldn't be safe to assume that. I have thought it would be a suicide job."

"Suicide?" the Governor asked.

"I have thought it would be brought into the station by a man—or men—during the rush hour on Friday. That that man—or men—would set off the bomb, knowing they would die. Fanatics are ready to die for causes."

"So if the station was shut off, that couldn't happen?"

"Unless we're taken by the five percent I can't be sure of—and General Franklin can't be sure of."

"But if we shut off the station lives would be saved, even if they managed to explode the bomb."

"Lives would be saved," Mayberry said. He smiled, a wry smile. "Of course I would be there, and General Franklin would be there, and his men and my men."

The Mayor lit a cigarette and looked at his empty glass.

"Let's pursue this a little further," he said. "If we shut off the station tonight, we have to make some sort of explanation to the public."

"Just say there has been a bomb threat against the station," Mayberry suggested. "The public is aware that we get bomb scares all the time—airports, bus terminals, public meeting places. A bomb threat is nothing new."

The Mayor inhaled deeply on his cigarette. "Fanatics, you've said, Mayberry. You know my biggest nightmare? That these characters break the story themselves; force us to take a public position. Tomorrow Martin Severance, here, will be told where we are to deliver the money. That is to be your last contact, as I understand it, Martin."

"According to the man on the phone," Severance said.

"Let's suppose we close the station," Ramsay said, his voice dull with fatigue. He must have gone over this a thousand times, Peter thought. "General Franklin and Mayberry take over."

"And you declare marshal law and we put the Army in the streets of Harlem!" Danvers exploded.

"We do all those things," Ramsay said, wearily. "So nothing happens. How long do we hold that position? A week, a month? Eventually we have to go back to normal. Without the station in operation the city will be a shambles. We are forced to go back to something like normal. And then Martin hears from his chum again. Now they want fifty million—a hundred million, and they don't tell us in advance where the bomb is going to hit. Fanatics!"

"They seem to have us by the short hairs," the Governor said.

"We had hoped, at the suggestion of Mr. Styles, that by letting the press in on what faces us, we might add to the number of allies who might hear something, pick up a whisper that would lead us to a direct confrontation—in time." Ramsay raised his eyes to Peter. "I take it, Mr. Styles, there have been no whispers?"

Peter straightened his shoulders. "I find this a very strange meeting, Mr. Mayor," he said.

"Strange in what way?"

"We are all white," Peter said.

"God save us," General Danvers said. "You're one of those, eh, Styles? A goddamned do-gooder!"

"I like to think I'm being a realist, General," Peter said, his voice cold. "You talk about deaths from the bomb. You brush over, once lightly, the deaths in Harlem and a hundred other Negro ghettos suddenly engulfed in a white backlash. You're dealing with a threat leveled at you by people who call themselves Black Power. Black Power is a much-advertised and small minority in the whole Negro community. All Negroes are angry, and they have a right to be. But only a few of them believe that their goals can be reached, their civil rights guaranteed, their equal opportunities achieved, by force of arms."

"They damn well better not," General Danvers said.

"They are as much concerned," Peter said, ignoring the General, "over the prospects of bloody battles in the streets as we are. Many of them may wish the station would be blown up. That somehow they could be *heard!* They'd like to cry out to us *'Now will you listen!'* But they are as aware of the consequences as we are. They know that after thousands of people are slaughtered in a bomb explosion engineered by Black Power that the public attitude will be much nearer to General Danvers' than to mine. So I ask again, why aren't any of their leaders here? Why aren't we asking for their help?

74

Why aren't they here at this meeting where decisions will be made which will determine their futures as well as ours for generations to come?"

The Mayor nodded, slowly. "I think that's a fair question," he said. "We have tried to keep this crisis a secret, Mr. Styles. We have tried to avoid panic and bloodshed before the crisis moment actually arrives."

"You don't trust the Negro leadership?" Peter asked.

"Why should he? They're the enemy!" Danvers said.

Ramsay made an impatient gesture at the General. Danvers was beginning to get under his skin. "I have called for a meeting of the Negro leaders at Gracie Mansion at six o'clock tonight. I asked them all—the moderates, John Sprague who is the chief spokesman for the Black Power group, Lincoln Waters, a half a dozen others."

"You're going to tell them what's up?" the Governor asked.

"That won't be necessary," Peter said. "It's common knowledge in Harlem. Have any of you been up there today? They're waiting for the other shoe to drop."

"You know this for certain?" Ramsay asked.

Peter gave them a brief account of his visit with Nathan Jones. "He knew why I was there before I even hinted at it. You see how it is, Mr. Mayor? You can trust ninety-five percent of your people, as Mayberry said. But evidently someone who is in your confidence has leaked the story from the very beginning."

The Mayor kept his eyes fixed straight ahead. "I almost wish you hadn't told me," he said. . . .

Peter felt a kind of light-headed dizzyness overtaking him. He realized he'd been steadily on the go for some fifteen hours. He caught a glimpse of himself in a wall mirror and was shocked. He hadn't shaved since the day before. A dark stubble of beard and his eyes, red rimmed and sunk deep in their sockets, gave him a sinister look.

The meeting went round and round and seemed to come out nowhere. Peter found himself feeling a genuine sympathy for the Mayor. James Ramsay had to make a decision that couldn't be satisfactory to anyone. Danvers had made the Army's position clear—the hawk position. The techniques of self-protection, as outlined by Inspector Mayberry, were a less than cheerful prospect.

At a quarter to six the meeting broke up, to be reconvened at Gracie Mansion, the Mayor's home, after his session with the Negro leaders.

"You better get some rest," Jerry Marshall's voice said at Peter's elbow. The Governor, the Mayor, and the others were crowding out of the far end of the room.

"These meetings should have been held weeks ago," Peter said.

"They were," Marshall said. "Always the same. No final answer."

"While we sit here chewing on nothing, what's happened to Marian Sims?"

Marshall put a hand on Peter's shoulder. "Pike is the best homicide man in the city. If anyone can find her, he will."

"No more meetings for me," Peter said. "Waste of time."

"You go home and get a few hours sleep," Marshall said. "You won't be any use to anyone if you don't."

"If I was fresh as a daisy what would I do?" Peter asked, bitterly.

"I wish I knew the answer," Marshall said.

Peter took a taxi downtown to Irving Place. His hand shook as he tried to get his door key in the lock. He had left the apartment in the middle of the night, bed unmade, ash trays brimming, but Mrs. Palmer, his cleaning woman, had been in during the day and the place was neat as a pin.

His first impulse was to drop down on the bed and give up. He reconsidered. He stripped and unfastened the harness of his artificial leg. He hopped, like a wounded bird, into the bathroom. He lathered his face with a lime-scented cream and shaved, and then hopped into the glass-enclosed shower and turned on the hot water. He stood under the scalding needle spray, leaning against the tiled wall, his eyes closed. Slowly he could feel his muscle tensions slowly relax. Finally he turned off the water and came out of the shower. He toweled himself dry and hopped back into his bedroom. He sat down on the edge of the bed, picked up his phone, and dialed the offices of *Newsview*. It was simply to ask the night man to call him in two hours.

"I may not answer the phone, Ed. Pooped. Keep ringing until I do. It's essential I be up."

He lay down under a cool, clean sheet and began to drift away.

The doorbell rang.

To hell with it, he thought.

The bell rang and rang. In a kind of fury he sat up and put on his terry cloth robe. He hopped into the living room.

"Who is it?" he shouted.

"Mike Fallon, Mr. Styles. Me and Timmy."

"Go away," Peter said.

"It's kind of urgent, Mr. Styles. About the men last night—"

77

Peter hopped to the door and threw the catch. He turned away and dropped down in the big armchair by his desk. He reached for a cigarette and the desk lighter.

Timmy Fallon and his father stood before him, blurred.

"Look, I've been on the go since Timmy came in here last night," Peter said. "I'm not sure I can stay awake to listen to you."

"We've been waiting for you to come back," Mike Fallon said. He was a short, square-jawed Irishman who was usually full of jokes. Serious, he looked like a small puzzled child; like Timmy's younger brother. "Timmy saw you and called me. I came as quick as I could, Mr. Styles. You like me to make you some coffee?"

"You could pour me a drink of straight bourbon from that bottle on the sideboard."

Mike poured the drink and brought it. It burned as it went down.

"It's about the pictures," Mike said.

"What pictures?" Peter couldn't seem to focus on whatever the problem was.

"The pictures they brought to show me from police headquarters," Timmy's high, piping voice said.

"Mug shots," Mike said.

"You recognized someone?" Peter tried to fix his hot eyes on Timmy.

"The boy was scared, Mr. Styles," Mike said.

"Rightly so," Peter said. "You recognized someone and you didn't say so, Timmy?"

"I couldn't be sure, Peter. Honestly I couldn't."

" 'Mr. Styles,' you little jerk!" Mike said.

"Come on, Mike. He's been calling me 'Peter' since he was four years old."

"My old lady would have his hide if she heard it," Mike said.

"So she hasn't heard it. What about the pictures, Timmy?"

"There was one," Timmy said, wriggling inside his clothes. "It looked a little like the man who chased me, only not really like him."

"So he makes an identification," Mike says, "and it turns out to be wrong. Right or wrong, those mugs may be watching and they pounce down on Timmy. If he isn't sure, I say he should forget it. Only he won't forget it!" Mike's voice was angry, but his hand rested gently on Timmy's shoulder. Peter realized he was really proud of Timmy's stubbornness.

"What was there about the picture, Timmy? I know how it is when you look at mug shots. You begin to think you recognize a dozen people—only not quite."

Timmy nodded. "It was like that, except this one, Peter. It was the man, only it wasn't the man. Like much younger. Like maybe a younger brother."

"I don't want him parading down to police headquarters, with a chance they see him go," Mike said.

"You didn't tell the police this younger brother routine?"

"They kept saying I had to be sure, Peter. Was it the man or wasn't it? But I kept thinking afterwards," Timmy said.

"Thinking what?"

"They take the pictures when a man is arrested for something. Well, this man might have been arrested a long time ago. They might not have a modern picture of him. You see what I mean, Peter?"

"I do. So you want to look at it again and tell them what you're telling me?"

"But not at police headquarters," Mike said.

"There were probably a lot of pictures," Peter said.

"Hundreds," Mike said.

"But they were in like books," Timmy said. "There was a number on this book—13096."

"Good boy. Slide the phone over here."

Timmy brought the phone on its long cord. Peter dialed Jerry Marshall's home phone. A moment later he had the District Attorney. He explained the situation.

"I'll have someone there with those mug shots as fast as I can. Your apartment?"

"For God sake, no! The Fallons live next door, basement apartment. I've got to get some sleep, Jerry."

"Sure. If anything turns up I'll let you know. . . ."

Once again Peter slid down under the cool white sheet. He couldn't remember if he'd turned on the air conditioning. He didn't care. Oblivion came almost at once.

He came slowly up out of darkness. The phone was ringing. It didn't seem possible that two hours had passed. But it was dark. He fumbled for the bedside phone and picked it up.

"Hello."

Dial tone. And then the bell rang again. It was the front door.

Peter moaned. He reached for the lamp on the side table and switched it on. Someone had a finger on the doorbell and just held it there. Peter pulled on the terrycloth robe again and hopped toward the living room.

"All right, all right!" he shouted, angrily.

He threw the catch on the door and was almost knocked down by an explosive entrance. He struggled to balance himself on the back of a chair. A black army stormed into the

80

apartment.

A giant Negro, a good six and a half feet tall, moved into the center of the room. He had a mustache and beard, wore black glasses, and had a blue New York Yankee baseball cap pulled down over his forehead. His sport shirt, open at a muscular throat, was bright orange.

"Check the garden," he said.

Two of his men, also wearing black glasses and gaudy sport shirts, went out through the French doors into the night. Another man went into the bedroom which Peter had just left. Finally, framed in the doorway, was Nathan Hale Jones.

"I brought a friend to meet you, White Man," he said. His smile glittered in the lamplight. "I don't think you've had the pleasure of meeting John Sprague."

The giant in the baseball cap looked at Peter. "Put on some clothes," he said. "I don't want you embarrassed by being half-naked."

"What the hell do you mean by breaking in here?" Peter asked, choked by anger.

"You opened the door, dad," Sprague said. "Don't forget that. You opened the door."

The two men came in from the garden. "All cool out there," one of them said. He was slipping a switchblade knife back into the pocket of his tight pants.

"Better dress, Styles," Jones said. "Make you feel more equal."

A kind of fury swept over Peter. It was an old story; a kind of shame at having his mutilation exposed. It did make him feel unequal. He began his grotesque hopping toward the bedroom.

"Hey, man, that takes some doing," Sprague said.

Peter reached the bedroom and slammed the door shut behind him. He got to the bed, sweat pouring down him. He sat, and reached for the artificial leg beside the bed. He began fastening the leather harness to his knee and lower thigh. The bedroom door opened and Sprague stood there.

"Get out of here, you sonofabitch!" Peter said in a low, shaken voice.

"Now you cool it, dad," Sprague said. "Just wanted to be sure the phone didn't tempt you." The black glasses fastened on the aluminum and plastic leg. "Say, that's quite a gadget. Take you long to learn to use it?"

Peter was shaking from head to foot. He stood up, turned his back, and pulled on his shorts. Then he walked to the bureau, got out a clean shirt and slipped into it. There were fresh slacks in the closet.

"How do women go for that stump?" Sprague asked. "I bet they love it. They always go for something a little off beat. I'll bet you've got all kinds of tricks you can do with it."

Peter turned. His face was dead white. "You miserable bastard, what do you want of me?" he said.

"Don't flip your wig, dad. I was just trying to make lightly while you dressed. But I came here to talk serious. So let's join the others."

Peter had seen pictures of Sprague. He'd been arrested, in the news, hundreds of times. This was the man who preached arson and murder to the Negro community. In the pictures, this great gangling figure with the beard, glasses, and baseball cap had looked comic. There was nothing comic about him in the flesh. There was an explosive energy, for the moment controlled, that Peter guessed could inspire fear and also an almost hysterical loyalty. The total demogogue, Peter thought.

In the living room, two of Sprague's men were at the sideboard pouring drinks.

"Put that stuff down!" Sprague said. "We don't drink till we're invited."

"So make him invite us, Johnny," one of the men giggled.

"Shut your black mouth!" Sprague said. "We're here to talk, so let's talk."

Nathan Jones turned away from Peter's bookcases. "Nice collection of stuff," he said. "You don't read many Negro writers though, do you, man? Well, crises make strange bedfellows. Johnny has just come from a meeting at Gracie Mansion. He needs help."

"From me?" Peter said.

"The mayor of this city is a mealy-mouthed, cowardly crumb!" Sprague said.

"Let's not waste time with public speechifying, Johnny," Nathan Jones said. He looked thoughtfully at Peter. "Life is made up of making judgments, Styles," he said. "I made a judgment about you. You come out on the plus side in my book."

"How do you think I can help you?" Peter asked, struggling with his shaking anger.

"Truth is a kind of frustrating thing," Jones said. "You tell it and nobody believes you, and you burn. I told you a truth this morning and I had the feeling you half-way believed it. That makes you unusual."

"What truth?"

"I told you I had no idea who was putting the heat on the Honorable James Ramsay and the City Fathers. I told you there hadn't been a whisper that threw any light on the subject. You did believe me, didn't you?"

"Yes."

"You wouldn't believe Johnny here though, would you? You don't like his music. You don't like it when he pleads with our young men to get themselves guns. You don't like it when he urges us to burn down Madison Square Garden, or Columbia University, or Gracie Mansion. His thoughts are all black to you; black, and dangerous, and if you could, you'd turn your power on him and burn him out."

"I've thought of it," Peter said. "I thought of it very earnestly five minutes ago."

Jones grinned. "You see, Johnny, I told you he was an honest man."

"And I'd chop him without even thinking about it if it would help us," Sprague said.

"So much for the love affair," Jones said. "Now for the help department. Oh, we don't ask for anything for free, Man. We stopped asking a long time ago, all shades of us. Thinking shades. Because Johnny and I think different. But we aim at the same target. But asking has got us nothing for three billion years. Now we demand, and we'll get it one way or the other—my way or Johnny's."

Peter's hand shook a little as he lit a cigarette. "I haven't had any sleep to speak of for about eighteen hours," he said. "I'm dead on my feet. I haven't got what it takes to listen to a party platform. You want something from me, ask—or demand."

"First we'll give," Jones said. "Last night there was a protest meeting in Union Square."

"Are there any other kinds of meetings these days?"

"I just came from one," Sprague said, his glasses glittering. "The Mayor was protesting that we got him over a barrel. I wish we did."

"You want sleep, Styles, don't make wise cracks," Jones said. "You know about that protest meeting. Dick Sims was there. That's where he was coming from when those bastards caught up with him on the street. Well, we've heard a thing or two. The meeting was in an old labor hall down there. The main speaker was our friend Johnny, here. And when Johnny gets talking it goes on and on. It's like an old-fashioned revival meeting, only bloody. Most of the audience was giving Johnny the Amen. But in the early part there were a few hecklers. And there was Richard. Richard, I understand, made an impassioned speech."

"To sit on our ass and wait for the white man to throw us a crust of bread, when the mood hit him!" Sprague said.

"I guess Richard was hooted down," Jones said. "The audience last night was in a Johnny mood. Burn down the nearest hospital that don't have an entire black staff."

"You better ease it, Nathan," Sprague warned.

"Don't threaten me, Johnny. You need me. You need me to speak your funeral oration when the time comes. Let me get on with Richard. He lost the argument at the meeting. Johnny here was still going strong after one o'clock. Richard was sitting with a mutual friend; mutual between him and me. So Richard said to this friend: 'I think I better call Marian. She didn't want me to come to this meeting. She'll be worrying.' So he left his seat to go out into the lobby where there were phone booths. They are old phone booths. I guess the company got tired of mending 'em. Whenever there's a protest meeting someone kicks out a slat or rips off a door. There's no privacy in those booths, man.

"So our mutual friend, after Richard had been gone a few minutes, decided he had to locate the gents' room. Johnny's oratory had worked on his bladder, it seems. Just as he hit the lobby, he saw Richard come bursting out of a phone booth and start running like hell was after him for the street. At the same moment—seconds later—a white man charged out of the next booth. He looks around and gets a glimpse of Richard's coattails disappearing out onto the street. He lets out a shout and three other guys—white guys—come running away from a cigarette machine.

" 'Nigger bastard heard me talking,' " the first white man shouts at his friends. And out the four of 'em go, running after Richard. So our mutual friend goes back into the meeting and listens, enthusiastic, to Johnny urging 'em to burn down the Cathedral of St. John the Divine; but he has no enthusiasm for burning up a little shoe leather after those men chasing Richard. Later, when the grapevine brings him the news, our mutual friend says to himself, 'I'd know that guy if I saw him again—the one that came out of the booth next Richard.' So he screws up his courage and he comes to us." Jones paused. "We give you that, Mr. Styles."

"And do you give me this mutual friend, so he can look at some pictures—mug shots?"

"We might."

"There's a small boy who thinks he might recognize a man," Peter said. "He thinks maybe he saw a face among some pictures. He's going to look again. If Mutual Friend picked out the same face—"

Jones looked at Sprague. The giant in the baseball cap hesitated a moment, and then he said: "We'll give you Mutual Friend."

"So you haven't really given me anything," Peter said. "You want Richard Sims' killers just as much as I do."

"Especially since they were white!" Sprague said.

"Now I come to the favor we want from you," Jones said.

"We may be reaching way in from left field. We'd like to know—and you could find out yourself, or through your friend, the august District Attorney—is it possible that Martin Severance was getting a phone call from his telephone friend just about the time Richard came running out of that booth with hell at his heels?"

Peter felt his stomach muscles tighten. "You're suggesting that Black Power isn't behind this holdup of the city?"

"We're telling you!" Sprague shouted, as though something had given way inside him. "I ought to know! I *am* Black Power in this city! Would I ask for ten million bucks if I had this town by the ears? We need a hundred times that, just to live! Someone's using us, man, just to make a cheesy little killing for himself."

"Using our misery, our anger, our frustrations," Nathan Jones said, quietly. "Maybe they collect the loot, maybe they don't. Maybe they blow up a piece of the city, maybe they don't. However it comes out, the black people of this town, of the whole country, will feel a backlash we're frankly not ready to cope with yet."

"It's like crazy, man," Sprague said. "We want these men stopped just as bad as you do. And so help me, if I find 'em I'll chop 'em into little pieces and stack the meat in Macy's window. When the screws are put on the Mayor I want to do it! If I get skinned alive, I want it to be for something I did."

Peter ground out his cigarette in an ash tray on the table. His eyes ached. Every muscle in his body ached. Concentration was an effort. The concept that they were dealing with a criminal scheme that had nothing whatever to do with the black struggle for existence was hard to assimilate. Somehow he had to put pieces together that didn't fit.

87

"You know what's happened to Marian Sims?" he asked. Jones nodded, slowly. "We know what you know," he said. "No more."

"Those creeps in the hotel know what happened to her," Sprague said. "We'll take care of them—later. Right now we got more to figger than how to get even for a white girl who messed up a good man."

"It's the wildest kind of reaching," Jones said, "but if Richard did hear that white man talking to Severance, and if your kid and our mutual friend can pick out a picture, it's just possible—"

"Was this notion of yours presented to the Mayor when you all met with him a little while ago?" Peter asked.

Sprague snorted. "You think they'd listen to the idea it might be anyone but us, man? We're the villains of this day and age, aren't we? We'd naturally try to point the finger somewhere else, wouldn't we? The Mayor is a great man, man! Heart of gold, jaw of steel, head of mush!"

"You can't present him with anything at this moment but facts," Jones said. "He's scared out of his wits."

"And rightly so," Peter said.

"We got just a tiny little itch of an idea," Jones said. "You get an answer to a question for us it might help us believe in our own itch. Then, if your kid and our mutual friend should pick out a picture—" He shrugged. "We could be in business."

Peter picked up the phone on the table and dialed Jerome Marshall's home number. Betty Marshall put her husband on.

"Like to ask you to do something, Jerry," Peter said, "without explaining why just at the moment."

"Shoot."

88

"Will you ask Severance when he got his most recent phone calls? I'm particularly interested to know whether he got one about one-thirty this morning."

"I don't have to ask him," Marshall said. "As soon as Severance gets a call he checks with me. Hold on while I look. Note book here in my pocket. I know he was called about noon today. He was at the New York A.C., about to get himself a steam bath and massage. Here we are. The one before that was Tuesday afternoon—four twenty. Severance was in his office."

"Nothing early this morning?"

"Nope. What's cooking, Peter?"

"Tell you when I see you. One more thing. I've got someone I'd like to have look at those mug shots you're getting to Timmy Fallon. A Negro man."

"You sound like you've been working."

"In a way."

"Those mug shots should be on their way, with Pike, to the Fallons' apartment now. Can your man show up there?"

"Hold it." Peter covered the mouthpiece and spoke to Jones. "Can Mutual Friend get to the Fallons' apartment reasonably soon? It's next door."

"He can be there in five minutes," Jones said. "He's down the block in a car. We brought him—just in case."

Peter took his hand off the phone. "He can be there whenever you say, Jerry. Within five minutes."

"I'll have Pike call you when he gets to the Fallons'. I'll instruct him. Are you on to something, Peter?"

"I hoped I was," Peter said. "Maybe not."

"Phone calls don't fit?"

"Something like that. I'll be in touch."

"You're not in trouble? I take it there's someone there."

"Who's not in trouble?" Peter said. "No, I'm okay." He put down the phone and looked at Jones and Sprague. Two sets of black glasses stared at him intently.

"Doesn't fit?" Jones asked.

"No phone call at the time you hoped," Peter said.

"Damn!"

"There's still the mug shot. You may come up with an identification."

"Why the hell did Richard run?" Jones said, more to himself than Peter. "Why didn't he go back into the hall where he had friends?"

"He didn't have any friends in the hall," Sprague said. "Last night was *my* night, man." He raised his huge long arms above his head. "*You* got to stop it!"

Peter watched him, fascinated. This black giant, pictured in the press as a sinister torch bent on setting the cities of the country on fire, was making demands of God!

Nathan Jones was at the door. "Sorry we took your time, Styles," he said. "We thought we could get an answer we could trust quicker through you than any other way. I take it you trust the District Attorney?"

"I've known him for a long time. He's supported by both political parties. He's not a politician in the usual sense. You people evidently keep book on everyone. How does he rate with you?"

"Above average for a Whitey," Jones said, with a tired smile. He glanced at the clock on the mantle over Peter's fireplace. "Nine o'clock. In thirty-nine hours the city has to make up its mind to pay or go to war. The thing is they'll be fighting the wrong enemy."

"But we'll fight them!" Sprague cried out. "We'll fight 'em in the streets, and in the alleys, and we'll snipe 'em to death from the roof tops. We didn't choose the moment, but they'll remember us!"

Nathan Jones' white teeth glittered in a sort of frozen smile. "So help me, Johnny, you sound quite a lot like Winston Churchill." He looked back at Peter. "Thirty-nine hours. You think you could persuade your friend Marshall that he and the cops are looking in the wrong place for the blackmailers? The more he messes around with us, with the black leaders, in Harlem and Bedford Stuyvesant in Brooklyn, the more he loses any chance at all of stopping whatever it is is going to happen. Time is running through all our fingers like sand on the beach."

"You're convinced?" Peter asked.

Sprague's huge hands rested on Peter's shoulders and turned him around. Towering over Peter, the black glasses seemed to burn down at him. "They say there was a letter sent to this man Severance signed 'Black Power.' "

"I've seen a photostat of it," Peter said.

"All right, man. I am Black Power in this man's town and I didn't send any letter. I am Black Power in this man's town and I haven't talked to no one on any telephone."

"But it could be some crackpots in your community," Peter said.

Sprague's voice rose and seemed to explode. "What in Sweet Jesus name do you think we've been fighting for for the last hundred years, man? We've been fighting for promises that were made and never kept. But we've been fighting from so far down, man, so far below the average snake's belly, that it adds up to little things, like a water faucet that don't leak all night and drive you crazy, like plumbing that don't stink, like a little heat when the winter chill is on, like no rats to bite our kids."

"Like you go into a restaurant," Jones said, "and the service is poor, and you know it's poor because the waiter is no good, not because you're black. That's what we're fighting for. Like you ask for a room in a hotel and they tell you there are no rooms—because there are no rooms, not because you're black. That's what we're fighting for."

"Not to live in ghettos," Sprague said. "That's what we're fighting for. And you know why we live in ghettos? It's not because you white bastards hate us black bastards. If we had the money we could live anywhere. Whitey would sell me his own child for breakfast, if I paid enough. We live in ghettos because we're so god-damned miserably poor there's no other place on earth to live. Crackpots in our community? We got a million of 'em, dad! They go crazy from just living! But that's the point I started out to make to you. We got the word about that bomb was planted in the Commodore Hotel. That was no toy, they tell us."

"A complicated, highly sophisticated weapon," Jones said, his coldly quiet and reasonable voice a stark contrast to Sprague's fury. "It cost money, Styles. A hell of a lot of money. Somebody had that money to make a threat stand up. If that bomb hadn't been found there wouldn't be half the sweat there is over things, right? That bomb convinced the big boys that Severance's phone calls weren't a joke. So I ask you, Styles, do you think that bomb was bought and paid for by some crackpots matching pennies on a Harlem street corner?"

"There's big money in on this thing, man!" Sprague said, his mouth twisted in a kind of anguish. "White money. And we're being used to take the whiplash and keep your eyes turned another way. So they'll be coming down our streets with machine guns and hand grenades and tanks and riot gas, and they'll kill us like flies, and we'll kill some of them like the rats they are. But before they get all of us, before they get *me*, I want three minutes with the bastards who thought this up!"

"It could be," Peter said, softly.

"If we weren't convinced of it, would we be wasting your time and ours with less than thirty-nine hours to go?" Jones asked.

"You know where I should be, man?" Sprague demanded, his face close to Peter's. "I should be uptown, handing out the guns, and the grenades, and the knives and clubs and bottles we've collected so we can go down fighting! But Nathan persuaded me you might help; might get a few people in high places looking for truth."

Peter lit a fresh cigarette and his hand was quite steady. His personal anger had evaporated. He was thinking clearly and rationally once more. It made sense. It explained the complete lack of any lead from the Negro community, despite expert police work, overt and under cover. They could very well have been hunting in the wrong place. Peter looked at the two black men facing him, their eyes hidden behind glass that glittered in the lamplight. They were so different, Jones and Sprague, yet they were linked by the same cause. Peter was convinced they both believed in their theory beyond question or doubt.

"I think I buy it," Peter said. "But don't get your hopes up. I don't promise I can persuade anyone else in the time that's left."

"But you'll try?" Jones asked.

"Best I can." The phone rang and Peter answered.

"Pike here, Mr. Styles. I understand you got a man wants to look at these mug shots. Where is he?"

"He can be there in five minutes," Peter said. "Timmy looked yet?"

"He's just starting," Pike said. "There are a lot of them. Send your boy along. Who is he, by the way?"

"Believe it or not I haven't the faintest idea," Peter said. He put down the phone. "If you fellows want that drink before you go—"

"Save it," Sprague said. "If we have any luck we'll get roaring drunk together—if you can stand being that integrated, man. Some place where we can break things!"

The black army was gone. Peter stood in the center of the room, looking around him as though it was strange to him. Anyone, he told himself, could write a letter and sign it 'Black Power.' Almost anyone could imitate a Negro inflection on the telephone well enough to fool Severance. The Hotel Molyneaux came into focus—and the four white men Timmy had seen beating Richard Sims. None of those people, Fatso or Georgie, or Irving, could conceivably be agents of Black Power. It was like watching a scene change on stage; a turntable revolving slowly to present you with a totally different picture.

The doorbell rang again. Now what?

Peter walked to the door, opened it, and stood there with his mouth hanging stupidly open.

The young woman who stood outside the door was tall, dark and lithe. The simple summer print dress she wore accentuated a lovely, full-breasted figure. Her skin was tanned a deep bronze color. Her eyes were bright with a kind of warm humor.

"Hello, Peter," she said. It was a low, husky voice.

"Grace! Grace Minafee!"

"May I come in?"

94

"My dear girl—of course—please."

She took a step toward him. Her strong, capable hands rested on his shoulders for an instant. Bright red lips brushed his cheek.

"Dear Peter," she said. "I thought your friends would never go. I've been waiting across the street." She walked into the room, looking around curiously. "So this is where you live. It's like you; comfortable, not too orderly." Her fingers touched the typewriter on his work table. "I've wondered about this—if it steamed when you weren't using it." She turned. "Oh, Peter, it's nice to see you."

3

It had been two long years since Peter had laid eyes on Grace Minafee. That had been another time of violence, another time of protest. It was a story told in another place at another time.

Sam Minafee, Peter's friend, had met and married Grace when they were working in the Peace Corps in North Africa. It had been an ideal, a perfect marriage. And then Sam had been cut down by an assassin's bullet as he was about to make a speech of protest at a mass meeting in a little Connecticut town. Peter had come to Grace's aid at that time, a Grace he had never met, a woman shattered by the loss of her man whom she'd loved with all her heart and mind. He found her to be a woman of enormous courage. And he found himself wanting her so badly that it hurt. He couldn't tell her what was in his heart. Her loss was too fresh, too overpowering. And he told himself, bitterly at the time, that a one-legged cripple was no mate for this vital woman. Not even a whole man could take Sam Minafee's place in her life. Not at that time, at any rate.

There had been a letter of gratitude from her. Months later

there had been a short note asking for a letter of recommendation for some job. He'd written it, of course. He tried to remember what the job had been. Something to do with the government, as he recalled it. Slowly what he felt for her was buried—but not dead, he realized, as he looked at her facing him across the room.

"Don't stay in shock, Peter. I'm quite real," she said.

"How well I know that!" He pulled himself together. "Can I pour you a drink? Make you some coffee?"

"Not now," she said. "May I bum a cigarette? I've stopped smoking, you understand, so I just borrow."

He crossed to her, offered his cigarettes, held his lighter. His hands shook.

"Peter, Peter," she said. Cool fingers steadied his hand as she leaned forward for a light. She still used the same scent, something he'd never encountered anywhere else.

She took a deep satisfied pull at the cigarette. "Your first encounter with Johnny Sprague?" she asked.

Back to earth.

"You recognized him?"

"And Nathan Jones," she said.

"If you know them, why did you wait across the street?"

"I hoped you'd be a little breathless when you saw me, Peter. I wanted that all to myself. And in case you just said, coolly, 'How do you do, Mrs. Minafee.' I wanted that to myself. I would have been naked for a moment."

He reached out and she was in his arms, her warm lips against his, her body pressed close to him. And then she pushed him gently away.

"Damn you, Peter," she said, her eyes dancing, "why did you make me come to you?"

97

"Because I didn't think—" He reached out for her again, but she turned away.

"I've dreamed of this moment for a long time, Peter," she said. "And now it has to wait. Didn't you know that there'd come a time when I would want what Sam would have wanted for me? A man. Didn't you guess that the man might be you, Peter?"

"Grace, I—"

"This we discuss later, Peter, because there are things you have to do. That's the excuse I made for coming here. That there were things you had to do—and that I could help you."

"I think I'm going to pour myself a drink," Peter said. "You?"

"Please."

He remembered bourbon on the rocks with a dash of plain water. He made it for her and one for himself. He brought it to her.

"Now please sit over there, a little distance away," she said.

He obeyed. Sitting was good. He felt a little dizzy.

"Do you remember writing me a letter of recommendation?"

He nodded. "But not precisely what for. Government, wasn't it?"

"The one thing I knew how to do, Peter, was work with people. The Peace Corp days with Sam. The place where people need help was in the cities, and I wound up in Harlem, working for Welfare. You can't believe what it's like unless you've lived in it. Bad housing, bad education, no full-time jobs, *no concern!* I listened to the politicians, the great White

Fathers, saying we must 'meet force with force.' It's desperation they choose to meet with force. Well, finally I couldn't go on working for government; too little, too late, too much of a nothing. I have a small income of my own, and Sam's insurance. So I've been on my own for about a year, helping where I saw I could help, fighting officialdom for people who have no way to fight. I'm not popular with the city fathers. The Mayor knows me and so do most of his city commissioners. The Police Commissioner knows me well, and your friend, the District Attorney, has had me up on his carpet a couple of times. It seems I am suspected of violating city ordinances from time to time. I get things done sometimes without waiting for the red tape to untangle."

"I'll bet," he said. She was so damned beautiful.

"I've also made friends, Peter—among the people in Harlem. That's how I knew Johnny Sprague and Nathan Jones. I've made friends and they trust me. That's how it happens that I've heard the whispers for weeks. That's how I know what the Mayor is sweating over tonight. That's how I know what's happened to Richard and Marian Sims. I knew Richard well. Would you believe that I saw you walk up Lenox Avenue this morning to meet Nathan? That—that did me in, Peter; seeing you. I knew I had to come to you. But first to help; later will be the time for whatever there is for us, my very dear Peter."

It took an effort for him to sit there in his chair, sipping his drink. "I'm not sure that I know what it is I'm doing that needs help," he said. "I'm a reporter, an observer."

"Not you, not ever," Grace said. "You are a fighter, Peter, and you always will be. Nathan and Sprague came to you to persuade you that there is no organized Black Power behind the threat being held over the Mayor's head. Did they succeed?"

"They made me believe it was possible."

"Not possible, Peter—so! Whatever I might believe, I wouldn't tell you something was true unless I was certain. If there was anything to leak in Harlem, it would have leaked and I would have heard it long ago. What we have to do, Peter, is to find some evidence to prove it, and take that evidence to the Mayor and his advisers before it's too late and they massacre the wrong people."

The telephone rang. Peter got up and answered it. It was Pike, and he sounded jubilant.

"Both the boy and your Negro friend picked out the same face, Mr. Styles. There isn't time for me to let you guess. It's that guy Irving up at the Molyneaux. I'm on my way. Thought you might want to go. I've got a police car here."

"Meet you out on the pavement," Peter said.

He put down the phone and gave Grace a quick account of what was up.

"Can I go with you, Peter?"

He touched her cheek gently with the back of his hand. "You are not to be allowed to get out of my sight again," he said, "as long as I live." . . .

Peter and Grace had just stepped out onto the street, when they saw the red blinker on the top of Pike's police car coming their way. Pike leaned out the window. His eyebrows went up when he saw Grace.

"Well, well," he said. "Mrs. Minafee."

"Hello, Lieutenant," Grace said, giving him her wide, charming smile.

"Mrs. Minafee has joined the army, Pike," Peter said. "I'd like to bring her along."

Pike's smile was wry. "My orders are to cooperate with you, Mr. Styles," he said. "But I'd like to think I wasn't going to get a lecture on police brutality in the ghettos from the lady."

"It's a promise," Grace said.

"Hop in," Pike said.

They got into the back seat. Pike sat in front with the uniformed patrolman driver. He turned around to talk to Peter and Grace. "I take it the lady knows where we're going and why? Well, young Timmy Fallon was right. It did look like a younger brother, but it was Irving himself. Irving Miller. Your Negro friend picked him out quite separately and without any prompting from the kid. Our Irving was involved in a loan-sharking bit down on the waterfront about six years ago. That's when the cops took his picture. He served two years on assault with a deadly; paroled on a three to ten. No trouble since—until now." Pike's smile was grim. "It feels good to get hold of something that doesn't evaporate like fog. Irving is real, and Irving clobbered our friend Sims and probably his wife."

Peter was grateful for the feel of Grace's firm thigh pressed against his. Her hand reached out and found his in the dark. God, what a night for her to have come back, when he couldn't stop to tell her everything he felt for her that was suddenly straining to be told.

The police car moved north and west to the Molyneaux. A big black limousine was parked about fifty feet down the street from the hotel. As Peter and Grace and Pike got out of the police car, Jerry Marshall and Sergeant McComas got out of the limousine to join them.

"Good evening, Mrs. Minafee," Marshall said. "Peter is always full of surprises."

"Grace came to see me because she knows a lot about this situation, Jerry. I think she can be helpful."

Marshall looked up at the battered front of the hotel. "This may not exactly be a tea party," he said. "You knew the Simses, Mrs. Minafee?"

"I knew Richard well," she said. "I met Marian once or twice."

"A bloody and unpleasant business," Marshall said. He glanced at Pike. "Ready?"

"Let's go," Pike said.

The first thing Peter was aware of as they went through the revolving door to the dingy lobby was the steady buzzing of the telephone switchboard. There seemed to be no clerk on duty, and whoever was calling was being ignored. The lobby was deserted. McComas walked over to the door marked "Manager" and kicked it open. There was no one in the shabby office.

Pike's face had gone rock hard. Had the Molyneaux's crew been forewarned?

"The basement is Irving Miller's bailiwick," Marshall said.

"I'll take a look," McComas said.

"Watch yourself," Pike said, his voice harsh. "Cornered rats—"

McComas took a gun out of a shoulder holster. "Don't tell anyone I didn't take a lawyer with me," he said, airing his perpetual bitterness.

He stepped into the rickety elevator and it disappeared downward. Pike went around behind the desk and picked up the phone. The buzzing stopped.

"Sorry," he said. "Room phone's out of order." He looked at the others. "For Evelyn, the redhead on the sixth floor. What a dump!"

The elevator was coming up again. McComas stepped out and his face was the color of ashes. He moistened his lips. "You better come down," he said. He turned to the patrolman-driver. "You take Mrs. Minafee out to the car and wait there with her."

"You found him?" Grace asked.

"Yes, miss, I found him," McComas said. "You go along with Patrolman Roush."

"I can take whatever it is," Grace said.

"What is it?" Marshall asked.

"A massacre," McComas said. "Fatso, Georgie, Irving and a fourth guy. Stood against the wall and mowed down with some kind of automatic weapon. They'd sink if you dropped 'em in water, they're so full of lead."

Peter had an unexpected vision of a giant Negro in a blue baseball cap. "We'll take care of them—later," John Sprague had said. . . .

Whatever Irving Miller had done as custodian for the Molyneaux, it hadn't included anything about keeping the hotel basement clean. It appeared to be a dump heap for old cartons, barrels of trash that looked as if they had been there for months, legless chairs, broken mirrors. The one place where there was any uncluttered room was around the oil burner and three large hot water tanks. In one corner of the space was a cot where Irving, or his night man if there was one, could nap. Beside the cot on an upturned orange crate was a half empty pint of cheap bourbon whiskey and a coffee can full of cigarette butts.

Peter noticed these things in a split-second glance before his attention was riveted on what lay crumpled in front of the far wall. He felt Grace's fingernails bite into his wrist. There were four bodies, sprawled grotesquely. In addition to Fatso, Georgie, and the wanted Irving Miller, was the aging night clerk Peter had encountered on his first visit to the Molyneaux. The old man stared up at the ceiling with bulging eyes, through the green eyeshade that was still in place on his forehead.

The smell of blood was sweet and sickening.

"Might as well not track up the place until the Lieutenant's boys give it the treatment," McComas said.

"Must be twenty slugs in each of them," Pike said.

Shirt fronts were red and tattered except for Georgie. Georgie had gotten it in the face and neck, perhaps as he pleaded from his knees.

"There must be other employees in this rattrap besides these four," Marshall said in a flat, professional voice. His lined face looked frozen.

"Maybe not," Pike said. "The guests, so called, aren't offered much. No room service, no bellhops. Four or five old ladies come in to clean up in the morning. If there'd been anyone else on the job, we'd probably have found 'em here. Okay, Mac, put in the call to Homicide." He turned to Marshall, as McComas headed for the elevator. "Looks like they were brought down here at gunpoint, lined up against the wall, and slaughtered. How do you figure it, Mr. Marshall? Payoff for whatever happened to Marian Sims or her husband or both?"

"Or they knew too much about it," Marshall said. "No question about Irving Miller? The kid and Peter's friend both picked him out from the mug shots?"

"Without hesitation," Pike said.

"All right, Peter, who was your friend?" Marshall asked.

"Believe it or not, I don't know," Peter said. He found himself hesitating to tell the whole truth for some reason. "Nathan Hale Jones, Negro reporter and writer—I mentioned him to you?"

"Your friend in Harlem?"

"And my friend," Grace said, her voice a whisper.

"Yes. It seems a man, whom he didn't name, was at that Union Square hullabaloo last night with Richard Sims. Sims went to make a phone call, and this friend followed him a few minutes later. The friend saw Sims run out of a phone booth, with a white man chasing after him from the next booth. The white man, who must have been Irving, shouted at some friends of his across the lobby of the meeting hall 'Nigger bastard heard me talking!' The four men went chasing off after Sims. The friend lost his nerve and didn't sound the alarm. But he told Jones—or someone who told Jones. Jones told me and had this man available for Pike."

"He gave his name as Matthew Twining," Pike said. "Had a social security card to prove it. Said I could reach him through Mr. Styles. Said he had no permanent address. Since he came to me as Mr. Styles' friend I let it go at that."

"When he identified Irving Miller's picture did you tell him who Irving was or where he could be found?"

"I guess I did," Pike said. "I told him the man he'd picked out was the custodian at the Molyneaux Hotel. I asked him if he knew the Molyneaux, or was familiar with the neighborhood. I thought he could be mistaken and just picked out someone familiar to him in a familiar neighborhood."

"So he could have gone back and fingered Irving for some

of Richard Sims' pals," Marshall said.

It was possible, Peter thought. Mutual Friend could have reported to John Sprague. He didn't have to go anywhere. Sprague and his boys could have been waiting somewhere around Irving Place for him.

"Look on the floor around the bodies." Pike said. "The blood is dried already. This didn't happen a few minutes ago, Mr. Marshall. It's only about forty minutes since I let Matthew Twining go. I called you, picked up Mr. Styles and Mrs. Minafee, and came straight here. These guys got it long before that."

"And nobody heard a machine gun, or whatever, firing?"

"They were brought down in the cellar to keep it quiet," Pike said. "Hot night, windows open everywhere. With what's on television these days, you can hear machine guns in your sleep."

"Let's get out of here," Marshall said.

They took the elevator up to the lobby. McComas was just coming away from the switchboard.

"Boys on the way," McComas said to Pike.

Marshall looked at Peter and Grace. "Would a cup of coffee in that place next door loosen your tongues any?" he asked.

"How do you mean?"

"You're a lousy actor," Marshall said. "You haven't told me everything."

"Good a time as any," Peter said.

The coffee tasted like lye. Peter lit a cigarette and stared with distaste at his cup. Grace sat beside him, facing Marshall.

"I'm being patient, friends," Marshall said. "We've got about thirty-seven hours to go."

Peter nodded. This was a man he had to trust. He gave the District Attorney a play-by-play account of his evening. Marshall listened, his grey eyes hooded, chewing on the stem of a dead pipe.

"You bought what they told you?" he asked, when Peter had finished.

"You make judgments on people, Jerry. I thought Jones and Sprague were leveling with me. That was my judgment."

"They were telling the truth," Grace said.

Marshall was silent for a long time. You could almost see him trying to put the pieces together in his mind.

"It could be," he said.

"You read the Commission report on riots, Mr. Marshall," Grace said, earnestly. "It's not just poverty, and no education, and nothing remotely like equal opportunity. We're a country sick with racism. There are some who can't wait for the Army to move into the ghettos and wipe out the people there. Someone shrewd enough and tough enough would see how simple it would be to blame this holdup of the city on Black Power. And if it comes to a bombing, no one will ask twice if a single voice is raised blaming the Negro community."

"What about what's next door there?" Marshall said, nodding toward the Molyneaux. "Why should I believe anything except that Sims' friends took revenge for him?"

Grace sat very straight in her chair. "Suppose they did, Mr. Marshall? Does that prove that Black Power is involved in an extortion plot against the city? If Richard's friends are responsible for that—that massacre, it can only prove that desperate people don't believe the law will hurry to help them."

"I like to think we'll move just as fast on behalf of Richard

Sims as anyone else in this city."

"Perhaps you will, Mr. Marshall. You're one in hundreds—an incorruptible public servant."

Marshall inclined his head in a little bow. "Thank you, Mrs. Minafee. I think you're a very beautiful woman. That takes care of compliments for the night."

"She wasn't soft-soaping you, Jerry," Peter said.

"Thanks again," Marshall said. "So you two are convinced we should be looking for a criminal conspiracy outside the Negro community. Where do you suggest we begin? We're running out of time, friends."

The counterman came toward them. "Sorry to interrupt, Mr. D.A.," he said. "But did you hear the news? It just came over the radio. They're closing down Grand Central Station and two blocks all around it. Some kind of bomb scare."

"Anything else?" Marshall asked, his voice sharp. "Any special details?"

"Just that there's a bomb threat against the station. Something about the National Guard being called out to help the police keep people out of the area."

The Honorable James Ramsay had made at least a part of his decision.

"I don't think I blame him," Marshall said very quietly. "He's got to think of twenty-five thousand human lives as a starter. I don't think I'd have the guts to risk it till the very last moment. You can't close off that station and its environment in five minutes. It's a small city in itself."

"It's going to go by us before we even start looking," Peter said, bringing his fist down on the table.

"So where do we start?"

"You start at the beginning, even if there isn't time," Grace said. "It all started with a phone call to Martin Severance as I understand it. Shouldn't we begin with him, Mr. Marshall? There could be something he hasn't remembered to tell you about his telephone contact—a pattern of speech, a quality of voice. Something said each time that could be a personal idiosyncracy. Have you been into that?"

Marshall gave her a weary smile. "I think I like you better than I thought I did, Mrs. Minafee," he said. . . .

In the old days you could find a politician at one of the party clubs, playing pool and drinking beer with his cronies and constituents. Martin Severance was spending this evening of special tensions at the Chamonix, a smart and very dressy nightclub on the East Side. Marshall located him through the Mayor's office. All the key men in the city administration were to be on immediate call and went nowhere without advising Ramsay where they could be reached.

The Chamonix was a popular spot on hot summer nights. The decor was Swiss, with murals of the snowy Alps surrounding the tables and the dance floor. The accent was on cool. The clientele was expensive and a little gaudy. There were, Peter thought, enough jewels on display here tonight to ransom the city.

Martin Severance was dark and handsome in a white dinner jacket with a batik cummerbund and tie. His single shirt stud was a blob of amber.

Grace and Peter and Marshall had been restrained behind a velvet rope by the headwaiter.

"In here we look as if we'd just come off the boat," Marshall said, looking at Peter's tweed jacket, Grace's summer print, and his own wrinkled tropical worsted business suit.

Severance had come away from a large, round table where he'd been sitting with two other men in white dinner jackets and three ladies whose short, smart evening gowns allowed for titillating exposure. Severance looked a little flushed. He'd had a few, Peter thought.

"Something cooking?" He asked Marshall as he reached the velvet rope. Then he recognized Grace. "Don't tell me you've come to complain about dirty subway stations in Harlem, Mrs. Minafee?"

Grace had certainly made her presence felt in Harlem, Peter thought, pleasantly amused.

"Like to tear you away from your party for ten minutes, Martin," Marshall said. "Is there someplace here we can talk?"

Severance turned to the headwaiter. "Can we use Max's office for a few minutes, Mario?"

"Certainly, Mr. Severance. This way please."

They were led down a narrow corridor, past the gent's room and the powder room to an office. It was a small, windowless room, cooled by a steadily humming air conditioner. The walls were lined with autographed photographs of famous performers—Louis Armstrong, Sinatra, Judy Garland, Pearl Bailey, and dozens of others. The neatness of the flat-topped desk suggested this was not a place of business. This was probably where Max interviewed the customer who wanted an extension of credit or to cash a check.

Mario left them. Severance stood near the door, jiggling coins impatiently in his pocket. Grace sat in the chair behind the desk and Peter stood beside her. Marshall was filling his pipe from his yellow oilskin pouch.

"I hear on the radio the Mayor has begun to evacuate the station area," he said.

"Pressure was too much for him," Severance said. "It could raise hell with things, but I guess he had no other choice. I don't know what I'd do in his place. Probably the same thing."

"Raise what kind of hell?" Marshall asked.

"It won't be so bad tonight," Severance said. "But in the morning when thousands and thousands of people find they can't get into the city by train, or into the office buildings where they work—the Pan-Am, the Chrysler, dozens of others—the lid is going to blow off. Some of the biggest and most influential business men in the city are involved. They aren't going to be satisfied with the simple explanation of a bomb scare. They have to know that this is something way out of the ordinary. Jim Ramsay may have to show his hand, and when he does the secrecy is over, the whole story is out in the open. A thousand big shots are going to be screaming for the Army to move in on Harlem and Bedford-Stuyvesant. The known leaders, like Sprague and Lincoln Waters, are apt to be hanging from lamp posts. That's the kind of hell raising I mean, Jerry."

Marshall held a lighter to his pipe. "Styles and Mrs. Minafee are convinced that Black Power has nothing to do with the situation; that we are dealing with a criminal conspiracy which is pointing at Black Power to distract attention from itself."

Severance looked as though he couldn't believe he'd heard correctly. "But you saw the letter—a photostat of it—Styles."

"Anybody can sign anybody's name to a letter," Peter said. "This man has phoned you every day from the beginning?"

"Twenty-three or four calls now," Severance said. "I had one here not twenty minutes ago. He'd heard the news about the Mayor's action. He wanted to tell me it wouldn't help. The station would go up on schedule he said."

Grace glanced at Marshall. "May I?" she asked.

"Of course," Marshall said.

"When you talk to someone a great many times, Mr. Severance, as you have this man, certain speech patterns, personal tricks of emphasis, vocal ups and downs, are bound to emerge. By the way, is it always the same man?"

"The same," Severance said. His smile was bitter. "We're quite buddy-buddies by now—the bastard."

"Are there things he repeats?"

Severance shrugged. "He always calls me 'Mr. Martin, sir.' That's supposed to be an ironic imitation of how a respectful Uncle Tom-Negro would talk. He really winds up on that."

"Winds up?"

"It's very broad—drawled out."

"Anything else?"

"He uses Negro phrases like 'Cool it, man.' "

"You're behind the times, Mr. Severance," Grace said, smiling at him pleasantly. "My five-year old nephew uses the same phrases. It's Hippie talk, Rock and Roll talk. It's part of modern slang."

"He always gets in a song and dance about black grievances—you know the line, Mrs. Minafee. No education, no heat, no hot water, bad plumbing, no jobs—all that crap."

"All you'd have to do to pick up quotes like that," Peter said, "is to read *Newsview*, or *Life*, or any daily paper."

"There's a special Negro inflection," Severance said.

"Any different than a white Southerner from Little Rock or Atlanta?" Grace asked.

"Yes, it's different," Severance said. "You'd be just as sure

112

as I am if you heard him."

"Which leads me to ask why these calls have never been monitored?" Peter said.

"No way to set it up," Severance said. "We never knew where they'd be coming in. Like here—or at an airport—or at a restaurant where I was lunching."

"But why not someone to stay with you so you could both listen when the call came?"

"We tried that," Marshall said. "I had a man stay with Martin with a high-powered transistor tape machine. There was never a call while the man was there. It was almost as though they could see us!"

Severance nodded emphatically. "You take all the Negroes in this town, and add to them all the do-gooding whites and Liberals and Commies who side with them, and you can keep every important man in this town under twenty-four hour surveillance. There's no doubt they're watching me. I'm important to them. I'm their contact with Ramsay. We're getting down to the hair-trigger moment. They know I'm in here talking to you now. Some waiter in this club has made a phone call." He shrugged.

Peter felt weariness leaning down hard on him again. There was no place to go with Severance. He was convinced about his telephone chum. Nothing would shake him. . . .

Severance went back to his party. Grace and Peter and Marshall were in Max's little office. The Chamonix's Dixie-land dance band was thumping out dance rhythms.

Another hour had been wasted.

"There was a man my husband and I got to know in North Africa, when we were there with the Peace Corp," Grace said, breaking the silence. "He worked for a shipping firm

113

there; dock foreman, or something. He was one of the few Americans, and Sam and I used to have a beer with him. We got to be very good friends. He's back here now, in New York, working as a longshoreman."

"So?" Peter said.

"He might be able to give us some kind of a rundown on Irving Miller," Grace said. "I think he'd talk to me without any holdbacks."

"That's a police job, Mrs. Minafee," Marshall said. "You can be sure Pike, to coin a phrase, is covering the water front right now."

"Talking to a cop is one thing," Grace said. "Talking to an old friend is another. I've learned that."

Marshall looked doubtful. "What do you think your friend could tell you, Mrs. Minafee, that Pike can't learn through channels?"

"Cigarette please, Peter," Grace said.

He held out his pack to her, and his lighter. For a moment their eyes met, and it was secret, private, warmly personal. Peter wondered how he had lived all this time without her. Now her dark brows drew together in a kind of intense concentration.

"You're so much wiser about a situation like this than I could ever be, Mr. Marshall," she said. "You've faced the need to get information from unfriendly sources thousands of times. The places where there is any information that could help us are unfriendly—unfriendly to legal authority. The Negro people like Nathan Jones and John Sprague have come to Peter, a stranger, with their ideas rather than to you, the law. They see the law as their enemy. It shouldn't be that way, but that's the way it is. The waterfront is another tight little community, afraid of the law, afraid of the Waterfront

Commission, afraid of its own leadership which will kill a man as casually as it eats breakfast. You call these people up on the carpet, Mr. Marshall, and you know how little you can get. There's never a witness to any crime on the waterfront. That's an old truism, isn't it, Mr. Marshall?"

Marshall nodded.

"It's the same in the ghettos of Harlem and Bedford-Stuyvesant. There are never any witnesses to a crime, large or small." Grace flicked the ash from her cigarette into a brass ash tray on Max's desk. "Look at that clock, Mr. Marshall." She pointed to an electric clock on the wall opposite the desk. "It goes and goes and gets nearer to twelve o'clock on Friday, and we spend our time talking! I don't know what my friend can do for us. His name is Mike Kelly, by the way—Red Kelly. But I'm certain he'd talk to me without reservations. What could he tell me? The only lead you've got in the whole world, Mr. Marshall, if you buy our theory at all, is Irving Miller."

"And he can't talk," Peter said.

"The Miller connection may mean nothing at all," Grace said. "Whatever Richard Sims heard in the phone booth may have had nothing whatever to do with the main scene. Irving can have been talking about some pilferage job on the piers; nothing whatever to do with the big thing. He kills Richard because Richard has overheard something about stolen cargo, or plans to steal cargo. Red Kelly may know something about that and it will simply take us up a dead-end street. And there is another possibility."

Marshall glanced at the clock. "Go on, Mrs. Minafee."

"This city is sick with hate, Mr. Marshall," Grace said, earnestly. "I know the kind of mentality that goes with the kind of violence that's been leveled at the Simses. Take this

115

Irving Miller. The violent world of the waterfront is where he comes from. He lies low because of his history with the police. He takes a job as custodian at the Molyneaux as a cover. Maybe the fat man and his son have connections on the piers. In the course of this cover job, he becomes aware of the Simses—a black man living with a white woman. Hate simmers. Big phony moral build-up. Irving talks about his outrage to his friends. They decide to teach Richard and Marian a lesson. Nothing to do with the big scene at all, Mr. Marshall. Sick villains."

"And your friends from Harlem pay them off," Marshall said.

"Maybe. And that's a police case," Grace said. "But there is a third possibility. Richard *did* hear a phone conversation about the big scene. It *is* connected with the Mayor's problem. If so, Red Kelly may be able to point to Miller's friends. If we can find them, they may take us to the men who are really behind the threat to the city. It's one chance in three, Mr. Marshall, but it's worth taking."

Marshall spread his hands. "Go," he said.

"I don't know how to locate Red Kelly," Grace said.

"Oh God!" Peter said.

"If he's a longshoreman, he'll be registered with the Waterfront Commission," Marshall said. He reached for the telephone on Max's desk . . .

It was nearly two in the morning.

A wet fog had descended on the city. From the North River came the spasmodic sounds of ships' foghorns. Bells announced the hour of two. The streets along the river's edge were deserted. The piers reached out into the water, long black tunnels.

Peter and Grace stood across the street from a dilapidated brownstone. Grace consulted a slip of paper on which Marshall had written an address.

"That's it," she said.

The windows were dark.

"Looks as if everyone had turned in," Peter said.

Grace's cool hand rested on Peter's. "You stay here out of sight. I'll see if I can rouse Red."

"I love you," Peter said.

Her hand tightened on his. "Thanks to that I feel as glamorous as—as Elizabeth Taylor."

"She can't carry your laundry," Peter said.

"Sit tight, you goose," Grace said, and walked out into the deserted street to the front door of the brownstone. She stood there, obviously ringing a bell. Peter felt his muscles tense.

A light went on somewhere in the house. There was a long wait, and then the door opened and a huge-bellied man wearing an undershirt and blue jeans stood there, looking at Grace. Peter could hear the voices across the street.

"I'm looking for Red Kelly," Grace said. "Does he live here?"

"I guess he does, lady."

"I'd like to see him. It's urgent."

The big man leered at her. "Won't I do?"

"Sorry."

"Well—come on in."

"I'll wait here, if you don't mind," Grace said.

Reluctantly the big man closed the door and left Grace standing on the stone steps. She gave Peter a little wigwag signal and the okay sign.

It was a good five minutes before the door opened again,

revealing a big man with curly red hair. He had on a blue workshirt and tan army pants.

"Grace!" Peter heard him say. Then they lowered their voices so that Peter lost the next. They talked for a moment or two and then Kelly disappeared into the house and Grace came back across the street to Peter.

"There's an all-night lunchroom down the block," she said. "Red will meet us there. We're to take a booth at the back and order something."

JOE'S PLACE. There was a lunch counter with stools on one side of the long narrow room, and booths facing it. The counterman had on a white apron over a T-shirt and white duck pants. A red handkerchief was tied around his neck. He was sweating. One customer, an old man reading a newspaper through thick spectacles, sat on a stool. He was eating pancakes. The counterman gave Peter and Grace a deadpan, non-interested look as they headed for a booth at the far end. He came down to the end of the counter.

"What'll it be, folks?"

"A cheeseburger and coffee," Grace said, giving him her bright smile.

"I don't think I—" Peter began. Grace kicked him under the table. "Cheeseburger and coffee."

"Cigarette, please," Grace said. "Marvelous how I broke the habit, isn't it?"

They could hear the hamburgers sizzling on the grill.

"You tell your friend Kelly anything?"

"Only that I needed to talk to him," Grace said. "Obviously the big man was just behind him in the house. 'Long time no see.' 'Have you time for a cup of coffee?' 'Sure, I'll join you at Joe's Place, down the block.'"

The old man on the stool finished his pancakes, folded his

118

newspaper, paid up and went out into the night. The counterman, juggling two plates and two cups and saucers, delivered their order. Peter took a bite of his sandwich.

"You got any old tires you'd like to vulcanize?" he asked.

The street door opened and Red Kelly came in. He walked to the counter, without glancing their way, and appropriated one of the stools.

"Hi, Joe," he said. "Coffee and Danish."

"Coming up."

Kelly lit a cigarette and glanced around toward the booth. "Well, for God sake!" he said, with a big Irish grin. "How do you like that, Joe? People I know. Bring my java down there. Okay?"

He came toward them, his back to the counterman. The smile was gone. He stood by the booth, eyeing Peter.

"You didn't tell me you had a friend with you, Grace."

"A very good friend," Grace said. "Peter Styles."

Kelly's eyes narrowed. "Newspaper man."

"Just a friend at the moment, Red," Grace said. "Please sit down, Red."

Kelly slid into the booth opposite them. He had the brightest blue eyes Peter could ever remember seeing. His jaw was square. There was a jagged scar on his right cheek. A cargo hook, Peter thought.

"You wouldn't look me up in the middle of the night just to say hello," Kelly said to Grace. "Not that it isn't great to see you." His eyes narrowed. "I was sorry to hear about Sam."

"Peter is the one who rounded up Sam's killers," Grace said.

"So you got at least one gold star in my book, Peter,"

119

Kelly said.

The counterman brought coffee and Danish.

"So what's new?" Kelly asked, when the counterman was gone.

"A man named Irving Miller," Grace said.

Kelly stared at her, hard. "I got a question," he said. "Are you working for the cops, Grace?"

"I'll give you an honest answer which won't satisfy you," Grace said. "The answer is yes and no."

"Let's talk about the weather," Kelly said. He cut a wedge out of his Danish with a not-too-clean knife.

"You hear the news tonight about Grand Central Station?" Grace asked.

"Bomb scare? Sure." Kelly's smile was sour. "That's the rich man's part of the town. Up there they call out the National Guard. Down here they say: 'Kelly, they say there's a bomb in the hold of that ship. Go take a look.' No National Guard. No kook from the bomb squad. Just Kelly."

Grace looked at Peter. "I'm going to give it to you straight, Red." She told him the whole story; the threat to the city, the demand for money, the letter from Black Power. Kelly listened, his eyes very bright. Peter could see the muscles ripple under his shirt as he moved slightly. A powerful animal with more than average intelligence, he thought.

"You can't blame those Harlem cats," Kelly said. "You read what's going on in cities all over the country, and you can't blame 'em."

"We don't think they're involved," Grace said. "We think someone is using them as a shield; using them as fall guys for a private scheme to get ten million dollars out of the city."

Kelly sat very still for a moment, pushing at his Danish

with the knife. "So what has this got to do with Irving Miller?"

She put the whole story on the table; its alternative possibilities. Kelly listened, and his face clouded.

"I don't think I can help you, Grace," he said, when she'd finished.

"You mean you won't?"

"You've leveled with me," Kelly said. "I'll level with you. I won't."

"Why?"

"Suppose I could tell you who the other three guys are who were with Miller when Sims was killed. You pass the word—to the cops, to your friends in Harlem. Black boys come down here and start shooting up the waterfront. Cops swarm all over us. And it wouldn't help for you to know, Grace. You could put thumbscrews on 'em and they wouldn't talk. The cops won't kill them if they don't talk. If they should happen to be involved in this big scene of yours, somebody certainly would kill them, and unpleasantly, if they did talk. They know what will happen to them, don't you imagine? They'll know what happened to Irving. This part of town will be silent as a tomb."

"Thousands and thousands of people will be mowed down if we don't get to the truth of this thing, Red. Women, kids, old people. The Army will go in, whipped on by red-eyed politicians—"

Kelly's bright blue eyes fixed on Peter. "How much do you really care?" he asked.

"Enough to risk whatever," Peter said.

"And you, Grace?"

She looked at Peter. "Peter and I are one," she said.

"Two gold stars," Kelly said, looking down at his mutilated

Danish. "What you two need is education. You think the Honorable James Ramsay runs this town? Or his commissioners, or the City Council, or your friend the District Attorney? You think the cops do anything more than catch the little fish?"

"You're saying—?"

"I'm asking," Kelly said. "Do the cops stop the flow of narcotics into this town? Oh, they grab the little pushers, and the hopped-up kids who mug the orderly citizens to get the dough for a fix. But they don't stop the—the importers. Because they don't know who the big guys are? Of course they know, but they're hamstrung because they can't get any legal evidence. They can't get evidence, and there's money poured out into the low levels, and the high levels, and there's pressure applied. Take it from me, this city isn't run by the names on the office doors in City Hall. It's run by what is popularly called the Syndicate. And, kids, it's *run!*"

"Name some names," Peter said.

"Ask your friend the District Attorney," Kelly said. "He knows all the names."

"Ten million dollars would do next to nothing for the people in Harlem," Grace said. "Ten million dollars in a private pocket is a lot of money."

"Grace, listen to me," Kelly said, earnestly. "Get out of here. Forget it. There's no way you can buck this. If you're right, and someone who runs this part of town is behind this blackmail thing, you haven't got a chance. If you even talk about it too much, you'll wind up the way Irving Miller did, with a stomach full of lead. Get intelligent, go away, get married. Live your own lives. You can't stop anything that's going to happen."

"Everybody lives their own lives," Grace said. "Everybody lets things happen. And then it spills over into mass horror."

"So worry about your own breakfast coffee, your own three squares. You haven't got what it takes. You're fighting out of your class."

Grace drew a deep breath. "If you would, could you tell us who Irving Miller's three friends were?"

"If I didn't care anything about you, I could find out," Kelly said.

"If you would, could you tell us who they are working for?"

"If I didn't care anything about you."

"Please, Red!"

Kelly stood up. "Sorry, doll," he said. "What you're asking I wouldn't do to my worst enemy." He turned to go.

The door to Joe's Place opened and half a dozen men came in. They were all dressed in dark business suits. They weren't longshoremen or seamen.

Kelly sat down. His mouth was a straight, hard slit. "Start eating your rubber sandwich," he said, sharply. "Talk to me. Laugh at me."

Two of the men came down the aisle toward the booth. The other four stayed by the door. Peter felt the small hairs rising on the back of his neck.

The first of the two men was lean, white faced, with little shoe button black eyes. The bulge under his coat was obvious.

"How you doing, Red?" he asked.

"Fine," Kelly said. "How you doin', Gadget?"

"Who are your friends?"

"People I know from way back," Kelly said. "This is Gadget Mullins, folks."

"Mrs. Grace Minafee and Mr. Peter Styles," Gadget said. "Friends of the District Attorney. You just left him a while ago at the Chamonix, didn't you, folks?"

Peter nodded. There was no point in denying it. The man knew.

"Friend of mine wants to talk to you," Gadget said. "You too, Red. My friend doesn't like loose mouths. So on your feet—like now!"

Peter glanced at his watch. Thirty-three hours to go.

PART THREE

1

Red Kelly walked to the door of Joe's Place without looking back. Two of the men stationed there fell in beside him and they went out onto the dark street.

Peter and Grace stood up. Peter remembered the small hand gun in the pocket of his tweed jacket. He expected to be promptly frisked for weapons, but he wasn't. Gadget Mullins' little black eyes were fixed on him intently, but he made no move to search Peter. Grace's fingers touched his hand.

"Shall we go?" she said.

He knew what she was thinking. They had gotten her friend Kelly into this mess. They had to see it through. At the front door the two men waiting there went out onto the street. Peter and Grace followed, with Gadget Mullins and the fourth man behind them. Peter saw Kelly and his escorts half way across the wide avenue toward one of the piers. From the overhead ramp he could hear an occasional car wheeling along the West Side Highway.

The fog had settled down like a heavy blanket. Kelly and his escorts were almost out of sight when they reached the other side of the street.

"Just follow the two guys in front of you," Gadget Mullins said.

Out on the river the foghorns bleated anxiously. As they approached the open mouth of the pier Peter could see the fog-shrouded superstructure of a big freighter docked there. Two widely separated portholes were lit.

Peering into the gloom Peter could no longer see Kelly. He and his friends had evidently walked into the pier. There was a watchman's booth near the entrance, but there was no one in it. He heard a long, low off-key whistle, quite near him in the darkness. A moment later it was echoed somewhere down the pier. Their approach was being signaled. A naked light bulb, suspended from the ceiling, glared at them from about fifty yards down the pier.

Off to the right there came a sound like a sliding door being shoved open. Instantly a second bare bulb popped on and Peter could see a large freight elevator. Kelly and his two friends had stepped to the rear of it. They followed. Nine of them in the car hardly took up any of the available space. One of the men slid the door closed and the car started up.

Peter glanced at Grace. She was staring straight ahead at the closed door. Kelly was watching her too. His Irish face was twisted into an expression of sardonic surrender. "This is what you get for helping a friend," it said.

The elevator stopped and the door was opened. Almost directly across from them was the frosted glass door of an office with light behind it. Once again Peter heard the low whistle, and its response from further away.

"That office over there," Mullins said.

There was no name on the frosted glass. Mullins lead the

126

way now and he rapped on the door with his fist. It was promptly opened by another business-suited character. He and Mullins didn't speak. Mullins stood to one side and gestured them to come on.

The room inside was large and bare. There was a commercial calendar on the wall with some Playboy art work. There was a wooden table with nothing on it but a man's hat, a black fedora. Behind the table, a man sat in a straight-backed kitchen chair. There were no other chairs in the room. The only illumination came from a green-shaded drop light that hung directly over the table and shone on the head and face of the man sitting there. He was a small man with thick black hair and shaggy black eyebrows. He was wearing black glasses that hid his eyes. His hands, folded in front of him were strong and used to work. He was wearing a pale grey tropical worsted suit, expensively tailored. His shoes, which Peter could see under the table, were blue suede. His smile was as wide and white as a toothpaste ad.

"Good evening, Mrs. Minafee—Mr. Styles," he said. "My name is G. Bailey Thoms. You, perhaps, have heard of me."

Peter had heard. This man was mentioned from time to time as a big operator in the city's crime syndicate. He had appeared before several Grand Juries without ever being hit with an indictment. That white smile was familiar. "G. Bailey Thoms on the courthouse steps, talking to reporters after the Grand Jury failed to take action against him." "G. Bailey Thoms, acquitted on charges of income tax evasion." There had been rumors of a Mafia connection. His real name was Giovanni Bailey Thomassino. The 'Bailey' came from an Irish mother. G. Bailey Thoms was said to be the king of the Manhattan waterfront, among other things.

"I trust you had no objection to coming to see me," Thoms said.

Peter had the sudden image of the Irish mother saying, "You learn to speak English good, Giovanni, or you'll get the back of my hand!" It was stilted, and yet it flowed easily.

"Would it have done us any good to object?" Peter asked.

"My dear Mr. Styles, didn't Gadget make it clear it was an invitation, not a command performance?"

"You mean we can walk out of here now, without being stopped?"

"Of course you can, Mr. Styles. My men will escort you to the first taxi to be found." His smile widened, if that was possible. "Of course, Red Kelly will stay with us. Red is part of our world, you see."

"A hostage against our good behavior?"

"You said that, Mr. Styles, not me." Thoms took a morocco-leather cigar case from his pocket. "I still get these from Cuba, Mr. Styles. Join me?"

"No thanks."

"I hope you don't mind if I indulge myself, Mrs. Minafee."

"Be my guest," Grace said.

Thoms took a cigar from his case, punctured the end of it with something that looked like a gold toothpick, and lit it with a gold lighter.

"I'm sorry there are no chairs," he said. "This is not my office, you understand. I—I borrowed it from a friend." He inhaled on the cigar, obviously pleased with himself. "I understand you have come down into my part of the world to ask questions, Mrs. Minafee, Mr. Styles. It seemed only

128

courteous to me you should have the opportunity to ask your questions of someone who has all the answers. Me." He looked at them like a small, eager child. "Please don't stand on formality. Ask away."

Grace's smile was bland. "Did you have a man named Irving Miller killed tonight?" she asked.

You could almost feel the dark figures in the background grow tense. Peter would have given anything to see Thoms' eyes. His face remained a smiling mask. He turned his head slightly. "Do we know an Irving Miller, Gadget?"

"We knew him," Mullins said.

"He's dead?"

"He's dead," Mullins said.

"He wasn't dead last night," Peter said. "He killed a Negro man on Irving Place; he and three friends of his."

"That's a bad thing to do with the climate the way it is," Thoms said. He hesitated a moment. "What made you think I might know Irving Miller?"

"He was waterfront," Peter said. "Strong-arm man for loan sharks. Served two years of a three-to-ten year sentence."

"Oh," Thoms said. "That Irving Miller."

"Yes, that Irving Miller."

Thoms studied the end of his cigar. "Is he the one who was wiped earlier tonight in the Molyneaux Hotel, Gadget?"

"Yeah," Gadget said.

"Bad place, the Molyneaux," Thoms said. "You know what happened there tonight, Mr. Styles?"

"We saw the results."

"Not Mrs. Minafee?" Thoms said, in a shocked voice.

"Mrs. Minafee. It wasn't pretty."

"I should think not," Thoms said. He hesitated. "As I implied, the Molyneaux is a bad place. Does your friend

Marshall know that it was one of the chief depots for distributing drugs on the West Side?"

"He didn't mention it."

"You tell him, as a little gift from me, that if he looks hard enough he ought to find quite a cache of heroin there. I'd like him to know it was me who tipped you off."

"I'm sure he'll send you a thank-you note," Peter said.

White teeth tightened ever so slightly on the cigar end. "Should we get down to the meat on the bone, Mr. Styles? Neither you nor I got time to fool around with the Irving Millers." He glanced at a fancy wrist watch. "Only a little more than thirty-two hours. Right?"

Peter felt his stomach do a little flip-flop.

"Do I surprise you, Mr. Styles?"

"By coming out in the open with it, yes."

"A lot of people work for me in this town," Thoms said. "One of them is Mario, the maitre d' at the Chamonix. Did you notice the little box on Max's desk? Intercom. Mario listened to all you had to say in there. He thought I ought to know about it."

So he knew the gist of their conversation with Severance, and Grace's theory that they might find the truth down here on the waterfront. Grace was standing very straight and still. Thoms had been waiting for them. No problem. He knew they'd be headed for Red Kelly's address.

"You're a smart woman, Mrs. Minafee," Thoms said. "Full of smart ideas." It wasn't said angrily. He seemed to mean it, as a genuine compliment. "You had some guesses you made about Irving Miller. Would you let me make a guess, an educated guess?"

"Please," Grace said.

"They tell me," Thoms said, his smile slightly twisted,

"that a major part of the supply of narcotics coming into this city comes in through the port, smuggled in in all kinds of ingenious ways. It's a big business, Mrs. Minafee—a billion dollar business. Some men working around the waterfront could well be involved—like Irving Miller, say. We have reason to think so, don't we, since he was connected with the Molyneaux. Now I can tell you from experience, Mrs. Minafee, that in any big operation that is run by manpower you have to deal with the unexpected. Human beings always do the unexpected. When I hire a man to do a job can I know always, in advance, that he hates women, or that he is a sexual pervert, or that he thinks he is better than the Polish guy working next to him, or the Irishman, or—or the Negro? I don't know till it shows up some way. Now how could any one know that Irving Miller would take a moral attitude about a black man living with a white woman? That he would decide to be a judge, to be God? But that's the way it—it could have been. So he's following this Richard Sims around, planning to bring down the wrath of God on him."

"You know the Negro's name was Richard Sims?" Peter said. "It hasn't been released to the news media—his name."

"Didn't you mention it?" Thoms asked blandly. "Well, I must have heard it somewhere. So Irving Miller goes to where Richard Sims is making a speech, along with some others. He calls a friend and says 'Tonight is it. We'll get Sims on his way home, and we'll get his wife later.' And Sims hears him and runs, but too late. And so they get Sims, and the next day they get his wife. You tell your friend the D.A. I don't think he'll ever find Mrs. Sims. I'm just guessing, of course, but I think she could have been chopped up and thrown into one of

131

those newfangled garbage trucks that would chop her up even finer. Fishes have got her out in the bay, somewhere."

Peter saw Grace shudder slightly.

"All guesswork, you understand," Thoms said. "Well, the people Irving Miller was working for, the people in the drug business, you understand, know they've got a dangerous maniac on their hands. So they get rid of him—and his friends and associates—quick. You can tell your friend, the D.A., he'll be wasting time looking for Miller's three collaborators in the murder of Sims. They've been taken care of, too. I'm only guessing, you understand, but tell Marshall I don't often guess wrong." He knocked the ash from his cigar. "So the Miller part of this thing is all cleared up."

"If you've guessed right," Peter said. His face felt frozen.

"Yeah, if I guessed right," Thoms said. "But like I said, I seldom guess wrong, Mr. Styles."

"Which brings us to—?"

"Why I invited you here to talk," Thoms said. He looked at Grace and the quality of his smile was now patient. "It is your theory, Mrs. Minafee, that somebody in my world is pointing a gun at the Mayor's head for ten million miserable dollars. Right?"

"It occurred to me," Grace said.

"And the next thing that will happen is that the District Attorney and the police force and the Justice Department will come swarming down here looking for someone who is pointing a gun at the Mayor. You see what I mean? If they decide to buy your theory, Mrs. Minafee, all hell can break loose in my world. I don't want that to happen. Now you and Mr. Styles come down here to ask some questions of Red Kelly, here, about Irving Miller—and about who might be holding a gun at the mayor's head. Now, unless Red filled you with a lot of his wild Irish imaginings, you have nothing to go on."

"Red told us nothing," Grace said, "except that we were asking for trouble."

"Trouble?" Thoms laughed. "You and Mr. Styles are as safe down here as if you were at a Sunday School picnic. You're friends of the D.A.'s, aren't you? He got Red's address for you, didn't he, and he knew you were coming down here, didn't he? How safe would you want to be, Mrs. Minafee?" Cigar smoke drifted around his head like a grotesque halo. "So you're our guest, Mrs. Minafee. So let us help you the best we can. We've taken care of Irving Miller for you, haven't we? An educated guess, right? Now about the man who's giving the mayor trouble. You'd like to know about him?"

"We would," Grace said.

"So would I," Thoms said, and for the first time the smile left his face. The reflection of two tiny light bulbs showed in his black glasses, about where the pupils of his eyes should have been. "I would like like hell to know, Mrs. Minafee. Shall I tell you why?"

"Please."

"I grew up in this neighborhood, Mrs. Minafee; a little wop kid starting from scratch. I worked on the piers. I did all right. I finally got in the importing business, G. Bailey Thoms, Importer and Exporter. There's other kids that grew up in the neighborhood who really hit it big. Not legal, but big. Like I told you, Mrs. Minafee, the narcotics trade in this town is a billion dollar business. Oh, I can see you disapprove. There were people who disapproved of liquor in the old days, but the people drank all the same. Well, I don't want to argue the point with you. But I'm talking about a billion dollar business. What makes it run smooth? No trouble. If we had big trouble, Mrs. Minafee, what do you think it would cost us?"

"You're talking about your friends who made it big, not G. Bailey Thoms, Importer and Exporter," Grace said.

"Sure," Thoms said. "I'm talking about the neighborhood. If we had big trouble it would cost us ten million dollars a *day*, Mrs. Minafee. There's no one down here pointing a gun at the Mayor, Mrs. Minafee—not for ten million lousy dollars. It's started already—the trouble. Tomorrow morning when nobody can't come in to Grand Central or the office buildings up there—BONG! Some screwy general will persuade the Mayor to start rolling the tanks into Harlem and then we've got like a war. You think we want trouble in Harlem? There are thousands of people up there paying a couple of bucks a day for a watered-down fix. That's big business, Mrs. Minafee. We don't want it disturbed."

"It's pure and simple murder, Mr. Thoms," Grace said, coldly. "I've seen the results of the drug traffic up there."

Thoms made an impatient gesture. "The people want it; they need it," he said. "But I don't want to argue that with you. I'm trying to level with you about your trouble. You're wasting your time looking for some kind of a conspiracy against the city down here. We like the city the way it is. It runs nice and easy. If I could make an educated guess right now on who's behind this, you wouldn't have any more trouble."

"Up against the wall, like Irving Miller?" Peter asked.

Thoms' real feelings began to show. "You don't talk nice for someone who's being done a favor," he said. His teeth bit down hard on what was left of the cigar. "I go with you," he said. "I don't think this trouble starts in Harlem, in spite of the way Johnny Sprague talks in public. I know it isn't down here."

"Where would you look if you wanted to look?" Grace asked.

"I'd look for somebody who needs ten million bucks," Thoms said. "It's chicken feed to hold up a city for. From what I hear they already spent a couple of hundred g's for that crazy bomb that didn't go off. Oh, don't look surprised, Mr. Styles. I'm well informed. You got any more questions? If not, my boys'll find a taxi for you."

"Does Red go with us?" Grace asked, glancing at her friend Kelly.

Thoms hesitated. "Sure, Red can go with you," he said. The black glasses turned toward the Irishman. "We always know where to find Red if we want him."

2

Two of Thoms' men went out to the elevator with Grace and Peter and Red Kelly. Once again Peter heard that long low whistle somewhere in the darkness, and its distant echo. The apparently deserted pier was very much alive.

The elevator jolted them down to the street level, and they walked slowly toward the mouth of the pier, the single light bulb behind them now. Up on the moored freighter, the ship's bell chimed.

There was a man in the watchman's booth at the mouth of the pier now. Peter recognized him. He was the elderly pancake eater from Joe's Place. He paid no attention to their exit onto the street. As if by magic a taxicab was pulled up at the curb. Thoms' man reached it first and said something to the driver, who nodded. The cab door was opened.

"Goodnight," Thoms' man said.

Grace looked at Red Kelly. "Come with us, Red."

Kelly hesitated. He was obviously interested in getting some sort of sign from Thoms' man. The man shrugged.

"Okay," Red said.

Grace got into the cab, followed by Red and Peter.

"Where to?" the driver asked.

"Irving Place and Eighteenth Street," Peter said.

Thoms' two men stood at the curb, watching the cab pull away. Peter started to speak but Red Kelly's calloused hand closed on his knee. He nodded his head toward the driver.

The taxi headed east and downtown in a zigzag pattern, the driver being an expert on the timing of the lights. There was almost no traffic of any sort. A few early milk trucks were out. The driver cut east on Twentieth Street, past The Players, south on Irving Place and east on Eighteenth Street. He stopped directly in front of Peter's door, an address he hadn't been given. He looked around with a broad grin.

"This do?" he asked.

"Rather specially well," Peter said, opening the cab door.

"I enjoy your articles in *Newsview*," the driver said. "I don't always agree with you, but that's what makes a horse race, no?"

They got out and went into Peter's apartment. No one spoke for a moment. Peter went over to the sideboard and poured three stiff bourbons on the rocks.

"That may have been the most extraordinary half hour I've ever spent in my life," Peter said, after he'd taken a full swallow of his drink. "Do you realize he as much as confessed that he runs the drug traffic in this town? That he literally told us that he'd wiped out those men at the Molyneaux and three more—the men who were with Miller in the murder of Richard Sims? That, in effect, he turned over a supply of heroin to us at the Molyneaux, just to convince us he was on the level? My God!"

"Molyneaux's no use to him any more," Red Kelly said.

"Swarming with cops. They'd probably find it anyway, sooner or later."

"Did you believe him, Grace? Or was he just trying to talk us out of something?"

Grace had dropped down into the big armchair by Peter's work table. She had lowered her head and her right hand was raised to her forehead to shade her eyes from the lamplight. For the first time that night Peter thought she looked beaten.

"I've been living the middle of Mr. Thoms' traffic for a year and a half," she said slowly, in a very low voice. "I've seen what happens to the people who are pouring every loose dollar they can lay hands on into his pockets. I've seen the anguish, the uncontrollable craving. The man is a monster!"

"You came out of it in one piece," Red Kelly said.

"He didn't have much choice, come to think of it," Peter said. "Marshall did know where we were. I should call him." He picked up the phone and dialed. Betty Marshall answered.

"He's down in the station area, Peter," she said. "He can be reached on the short-wave police radio if it's an emergency."

"I should talk to him," Peter said.

"I'll get word to him," Betty said. "Where are you?"

"My apartment."

"Sit tight," Betty said. "Are you listening to the radio?"

"No."

Betty's voice sounded frayed. "The whole thing has blown wide open. Dexter Calhoun is on WABA right now. It's scarey. Take a listen while I try to find Jerry for you. These are bad times, Peter."

Peter put down the phone and turned to the radio set on a side table. He hesitated a moment. WABA was a powerful small station, located somewhere across the Hudson, and openly operated by the ABA—Army for a Basic America. ABA was one of a number of crackpot organizations like The Minutemen, and The Soldiers of the Cross, secretly arming and drilling their followers for the day when they would obliterate our "communist dominated" government and take control. General Dexter Calhoun was known to be the Commander for the eastern third of the United States. Most people laughed at his charges that men like Presidents Eisenhower, Kennedy, and Johnson were communist tools, but there were too many who didn't.

Grace wouldn't laugh when she heard Dexter Calhoun on the radio. It had been a fanatical cell of the ABA which had ordered the assassination of Sam Minafee and carried it out.

"Sorry about this," Peter muttered, and switched on the radio.

"—a cowardly position that must make all true Americans shudder with disbelief!" Dexter Calhoun's deep voice with its soft, southern undertone, blasted out into the room. Grace's head jerked up. "For weeks the truth has been kept from the people of this city. For weeks a sinister plot to murder thousands of people in cold blood has been well known to city officialdom. What have they done? They have waited until the very last minute, doing nothing, hoping that by ignoring a crisis it would just go away. Well, thank God the truth has leaked out into the open and it may still not be too late.

"Tonight a great transportation center of this city is closed down, and tomorrow morning no one will be able to come or go into or out of the city. Tomorrow thousands upon thousands of honest working people will not be able to get to their offices, their places of business. A craven Mayor is now in his office, shaking with fear, prepared to pay ransom to communist-inspired black terrorists. *This must not be allowed to happen!* Americans never have and never will knuckle under to threats of naked violence. I look at the clock on the wall just beyond me. It is ten minutes past five A.M. The Mayor must surrender or face the consequences in less than thirty-one hours. He must pay an incredible sum of money for temporary safety—I say temporary, because, if he pays, it will only be a matter of time before a second demand is made, and a third, and a fourth, and God knows how many more. So I say to you we must *not* wait these thirty-one hours! We must not wait thirty-one minutes to take command of this situation. Armed forces are available to us. It is my understanding that General Danvers has troops and material of a military nature close by. We have a police force. And we have patriotic organizations such as the Army for a Basic America, trained and ready to fight for our freedom. I say this to you here and now. The Mayor should be removed from office, impeached, and made to stand trial for selling out to a communist conspiracy. Authority should be placed in the hands of a man, or men, who are ready to fight for our freedom. I say we should move now, in the early hours this morning, to wipe out the black terrorists in this city. I urge—no, I demand—that General Danvers be ordered to advance at once, immediately, to crush this rebellion now and forever!"

Peter switched off the radio. He reached out and put his hand on Grace's shoulder. She was trembling. The same voices of hate had nearly destroyed her two years ago. She must, he knew, be remembering the horror of looking down at Sam, lying on a Connecticut green, his face shot away. A counterpart of General Calhoun had been responsible.

The telephone rang.

"Peter? Jerry Marshall. Can you come up here? I think you should."

"Yes. How do I get to you?"

"McComas will be waiting for you at the corner of Fortieth and Park."

"On my way," Peter said.

"No, Mrs. Minafee," Marshall said, his voice grim. "As my father used to say, 'it's a man's world' up here."

"We just came from a man's world," Peter said. "She took that in stride."

"Any luck?"

"Some facts that may interest you. No luck."

"Well, get moving if you want to be in on the big one."

"Big one?"

"News story of this or any other year," Marshall said. . . .

Peter was startled to discover that it was quite light when he got out onto the street. Twenty-four hours ago he had stood outside the Molyneaux with Marshall and seen the red sun rising. This was going to be another scorching day. The street seemed oven hot, even this early in the morning, after his air-cooled apartment.

Peter had left Grace stretched out on the bed in his room getting the rest she denied, almost groggily, that she needed. Red Kelly was slumped in the big arm chair, chain smoking, with the bottle of bourbon at his elbow. He had agreed to stay with Grace "just in case." It seemed to Peter that people had come and gone in swarms during the past day. He didn't want Grace alone. She'd projected herself too deeply into the situation. Someone might want her stopped.

There was no traffic, no taxi anywhere in sight. Peter thought of trying to get his car out of a nearby garage but decided it would probably take longer than to walk the twenty blocks uptown.

He crossed over to Park and headed north, walking briskly. He was aware of a strange, unfamiliar sound which he couldn't place for a moment. And then, with a slight chill running along his sweat-soaked back, he realized it was voices—thousands of human voices, yelling and chanting. By the time he reached Thirty-fourth Street the sound of the voices grew loud and threatening. Normally there were very few people on the streets at this time. There were suddenly a great many, most of them headed north. People were in the windows of the tall apartment buildings, all of them staring uptown toward the station and the Pan-Am tower. There was the strange background accompaniment of the sound of thousands of radio and TV sets. The usual music programs were not on this morning. Commentators and on-the-scene reporters in mobile units were going full blast.

By the time he reached Fortieth Street, Peter was literally elbowing his was through a thick jam of people. He was wondering how he'd find McComas when he saw the D.A.'s special cop edge his way out of the doorway to the Architects' Building. McComas was wiping the sweat from his face with a handkerchief.

"Lid's blown off," he said when he reached Peter.

Peter saw that Park Avenue was shut off at Fortieth Street with "Street Closed" signs. The ramp around the station was closed. A shoulder-to-shoulder line of National Guardsmen with bayoneted rifles made a barrier across the street from building wall to building wall. Strangely excited people were jeering and shouting at them.

"You'd think if they knew the station might blow up they'd stay away," McComas said. "They're pressing in like this all around the closed-off area. If there really was a big blowup, there'd be thousands of 'em killed by falling masonry. The whole goddam lot of 'em are flirting with suicide."

At the barrier of guardsmen McComas spoke to an officer who quickly passed them through the line. It was clearly pre-arranged. Suddenly there were just two of them, heading down the hill from Fortieth Street to the station. Peter glanced up at the station clock. Ten minutes to six.

There were policemen on all the station doors, but again there was no problem about passing through. The station was strangely ghostlike. Their heels made a hollow echo on the stone floors. The waiting rooms were empty. The great mall with the information booth in its center looked larger than Peter remembered its being. Baggage rooms, lunch counters, shops, and ticket windows were all dark and closed. A polished red sports car on a dais that normally revolved, stood motionless, its doors open as if someone had just left it. From outside the chanting voices now sounded muffled and distant.

Jerry Marshall was in the station master's office. He looked old and gray, his eyes red rimmed. He was chewing on a dead pipe. With him were O'Connor, the Police Commissioner, Inspector Mayberry of the Bomb Squad, a young man Peter remembered from the day before at the meeting—one of Mayor Ramsay's staff, and the station master. This man and Mayberry were studying charts spread out on two large drawing boards. O'Connor was on the phone, obviously getting reports from Center Street.

Marshall gestured toward the charts with his pipe stem.

143

"We're going over this place, inch by inch," he said. "We should cover an awful lot of it, if they don't move up the time schedule on us. Track walkers are covering every siding and every inch of rail out into the open at Ninety-sixth Street. How is it outside?"

"Noisy," Peter said.

"Mrs. Minafee's friend couldn't help you?"

"Oh, we had a ball," Peter said. As briefly as he could he described the meeting with G. Bailey Thoms. Marshall listened, frowning.

"I guess we owe that slick operator a vote of thanks," he said. "I suspect he was telling you the truth. You know something, Peter? We're not any closer to putting our hands on the people we want than we were the day the first phone call came to Marty Severance."

"How did the story leak?"

Marshall shrugged. "Your friends in Harlem knew, didn't they? Thoms knew. Like Mayberry said, there's a five percent we have to trust who shouldn't be trusted. You hear Calhoun on the radio?"

"Bastard!"

"The problem now is not only can we stop a mob attack on Harlem, but can we stop the higher-ups—people over Ramsay's head like the Governor, or the big White Father in Washington, from turning General Danvers loose with his tanks and soldiers? It's a political year. They've all been hollering about 'crime in the streets,' but what they really mean by that is a black man with a rock in his hand."

"Who needs ten million dollars?" Peter asked.

"I do, for one," Marshall said. He looked curiously at Peter. "Why do you ask?"

"Thoms' advice. Look for someone who really needs ten

million bucks."

Marshall looked down at the pipe in his hand. "My whole career as a public prosecutor has been devoted to dealing with people who need money and will do anything to get it," he said. "That's what's at the root of almost all crime. The jails around the state are full of guys I put there, a lot of them for reaching for almost as much as is involved here."

"You didn't send for me to give me your Criminology A course," Peter said.

Marshall nodded and beckoned to the Mayor's assistant. The young man joined them, very Ivy League like his boss. "You met Paul Austin yesterday afternoon," Marshall said.

"We waved hello," Peter said.

"Nice to see you again, sir," Austin said. He needed a shave and he was self-conscious about it. "The Mayor asked me to talk to you. He thinks you can help."

"How?"

"Most of the city is glued to its TV and radio sets, Mr. Styles," Austin said. "Ninety percent of what's coming over tends to stir people toward unreasonable violence. The reporters out on the streets are only interested in the explosive areas. And there are a hell of a lot of them."

"So?"

"The Mayor wants you to go on television and radio, Mr. Styles," Austin said.

"People know you and your attitude toward this kind of thing," Marshall said. "Millions of them read your column in *Newsview*."

"I'm flattered but I doubt I could be very effective," Peter said.

Austin rubbed at the stubble on his chin. "Up all night," he said apologetically. "No chance to shave. What the Mayor hopes is that someone can throw some doubt on the general conviction that the city is being threatened by Black Power. I understand that is what you believe?"

"I think I believe that," Peter said, slowly.

"You're not a politician, Mr. Styles. You don't have to please voters, or the City Council, or anyone else. You have a reputation for being concerned only with the truth. If you would go on the air and say that you are convinced that Black Power isn't at the bottom of this bombing threat, it might help to stem the tide. You could make a tape that could be shown at frequent intervals throughout the morning. We believe it has to be done at once. The hawks in this situation aren't going to wait till tomorrow unless enough people speak out against them. Will you do it?"

"If Ramsay really thinks it will help."

"Fine," Austin said. "There are studios here in the station where the tape can be made. I'll get things organized. Could you go on in fifteen or twenty minutes?"

"Strictly off the top of my head," Peter said.

"I'll have a cop bring Peter up to the studio," Marshall said. "And you better have Mayberry send a man with you, Paul." Marshall's smile was wry. "You might be one of the five percent."

Austin took off.

"I've got something else for you, Peter," Marshall said. "I told you I didn't want Mrs. Minafee up here. I had a reason."

"You always do."

"I want to ask her to do something," Marshall said. "I know she will say yes. So I wanted to ask you before I asked her. I think I know that she isn't just a casual friend of yours."

"Not casual," Peter said.

"What I want her to do could be dangerous. If you think it's too dangerous I may not ask."

"*May* not?"

"Desperate situations call for desperate measures, Peter." Automatically Marshall began to fill his dead pipe. "You know what's outside here and what's on the air. It could explode any minute. White Power could go into action full blast while we stand here talking. But that isn't the only danger. Up in Harlem, John Sprague has gone crazy. He knows what is likely to happen and he's urging his people to strike first. If they are going to die, they should die in the white part of the city, tearing it to pieces. We know they have guns, and homemade bombs, and rocks and clubs—and hate! If they should move first, we haven't got a prayer of stopping a holocaust."

"What has this got to do with Grace?" Peter asked, knowing the answer before he got it, and resisting the notion fiercely.

"They trust Mrs. Minafee up there," Marshall said. "She has lived with them and worked with them for more than a year. If she could get to Sprague and persuade him that we're doing everything in our power to prevent violence; that we don't believe they are behind the threat to the city; that we haven't got a chance of stopping a disaster if he moves first. Sprague would laugh in the Mayor's face if he went up there and said it. He would laugh at any of us who are officials. He'd accuse us of trying to sweet talk him into holding back until we were ready to strike. He might believe Mrs. Minafee. He just might believe her."

"And the danger—what you think it is?"

"There are fanatics everywhere, Peter. Fanatics on our side, fanatics on their side. It's possible that a white woman trying to put a check on Sprague's demagogic hoopla might be—be treated roughly."

Peter stared at his friend. His eyes felt hot and tired. Every instinct he had told him that Grace should stay out of this. Under a full head of steam John Sprague wasn't likely to listen to anybody.

"You say Sprague wouldn't believe you, Jerry, or any other city official. Can Grace believe you?"

"Fair question," Marshall said. He held a lighter to his pipe. "We have a little more than twenty-nine hours to payoff time, if this isn't triggered in advance. No official in his right mind would authorize an invasion of the ghettos until he'd exhausted every other possible choice."

"Can you control the generals, and the crackpot generals like Calhoun?"

"We can control the Army," Marshall said. "Whatever General Danvers may feel about it, he can't move unless the Mayor asks for help. Ramsay won't ask for help unless Sprague starts things happening. If Calhoun and his goons attempt to move, General Danvers will find himself forced to use his men to stop a friend. I believe we can control things for another twenty-four hours, Peter, if Sprague is held in check."

"And how does Grace persuade him that he isn't wasting his best opportunity by waiting?"

"The possibility that we will find the real conspirators."

"Do you believe we will?"

Marshall looked steadily at Peter. "I wish I could say I believed we would. We've tried for three weeks without success. You've tried. You've eliminated, at least to my satisfaction, Black Power and the criminal syndicate represented by your friend Thoms. We don't have one shaft of light pointing anywhere else. We're now involved in trying to plug up a thousand rat holes. We have scores of men looking for leads. So far, nothing. But we're trying, Peter, with every facility at our command. If Mrs. Minafee can get Sprague to listen to reason—"

"I have a feeling he's past listening," Peter said. "He's been screaming for violence for so long that if he backs away now, when his people are ready to believe him at last, the power he's looking for may slip through his fingers."

"Damn it, Peter, we have to try!" Marshall said. His calm was balanced on a knife edge. Fatigue had worn him raw.

Peter knew one thing. If Grace was asked, she would go. What if the roof caved in and she found out later that he had prevented her being asked?

"Call Grace," he said. "I'd like to tell her that I hope she says no. But ask her, Jerry."

Marshall dialed the apartment and got Grace. He put the situation to her just as fairly as Peter could have asked. When he'd finished, he told her that Peter wanted to speak to her.

"I know what you're going to say, Peter," she said. Her low voice sounded tense.

"Do you think Sprague will listen to you?"

"I may not be able to get anywhere near him," she said. "When he's wound up, it's a performance. It's a little like trying to talk to an actor playing *Hamlet* in the middle of a soliloquy. But there are people who might help me—Nathan, others."

"Will Red Kelly go with you?"

"It would be a mistake, Peter. That's not a white man's town up there this morning. I have been a friend. I may still be considered a friend."

"Promise me one thing. Keep in touch. If I don't hear from you every hour or so—" He glanced at Marshall. "Call here. They can find me." He gave her the number.

"Dear Peter, I'll do the best I can, but it may not be easy to get to a phone. Don't worry too much. I'm a big girl."

"I'm taping a television speech for the Mayor," Peter said. "It may be on the air pretty soon. Try to get Sprague to listen to it. Some of it will be for him."

"Thank God, Peter. Most of the news people have gone crazy hysterical. Red and I have been listening."

"I don't know how it'll work," Peter said. "I'm normally a stirrer-upper, not a calmer-downer."

"I'll do my best to keep in touch," Grace said. "Because— well, just because—do you mind if I tell you that I love you, Peter?"

"Mind! Oh my God!" . . .

A plainclothes man took Peter through the empty station to a bank of elevators on the south end. The policeman ran the car himself up to the floor where the TV studios were located.

There were a couple of cameramen on the studio floor, and an engineer and a director behind the glass panel of the control booth. The director came out of the booth and down onto the floor.

"I'm Jake Potter, Mr. Styles."

"Hi."

"We set up a desk and chair for you. Okay? You may find

it easier sitting than standing. I suppose you got notes?"

"Off the top of my head," Peter said.

Potter frowned. "We have to be pretty precise as to time. Five minute spot according to my orders. That means four-thirty for you. Leaves room for an intro."

Peter felt a slow burn beginning.

"This building may come down over our heads before we're finished, and we must be exact about the length of this speech?"

"You know how it is," Potter said. "The networks will be giving up commercial time. Pre-taped shows are already prepared."

"Rome burns but we must go on selling our soap and cereal," Peter said.

"Sorry," Potter said. He looked at Peter, critically. "Maybe you should have a small make-up job."

"Skip it," Peter said. "They'll have to take me the way I am."

"Remember what happened to Nixon in sixty," Potter said, laughing at his own joke. "Just sit at that table, Mr. Styles. One camera will remain fixed. The other will move in and out on you to vary the picture. I'll be making the choice of which picture to take in the booth." He glanced at the wall clock. "We'll go at exactly seven o'clock. I'll signal you when we have thirty seconds left. We cut out at four-thirty after the hour. All clear?"

"You're a joker, Mr. Potter," Peter said. "Have you been out on the street lately?"

He sat down at the table, trying to compose himself. The cameraman facing him spoke. "When the red light goes on there on the face of the camera, you'll know we're taping, Mr. Styles."

Peter sat motionless, his hands covering his face. A voice came over the intercom. "Ten seconds to go, Mr. Styles. Eight—seven—six—five—four—three—two—one."

"This is Peter Styles, regular columnist for *Newsview Magazine*. I have exactly four minutes and twenty seconds in which to persuade you to save your lives and the lives of your neighbors. You all know that someone is blackmailing the city, threatening to blow up Grand Central Station and surrounding buildings if the Mayor does not pay a ransom of ten million dollars by noon tomorrow. You have been told by many loud and hysterical voices that this threat comes from the Negro community of this city, or a segment of it called Black Power. I have been working on this case for some twenty-eight hours without rest or sleep. I tell you, with all the conviction that I can muster, that Black Power has nothing to do with this threat to the city."

The left-hand camera was moving in close. Peter struggled to keep looking staight ahead, to keep his thoughts in one piece.

"I am broadcasting from Grand Central Station. A deserted station. I have seen the crowds held off by the National Guard and the police for a distance of two blocks in all directions from the place. I have heard them shouting, mindlessly, for a mass assault on Harlem and the total destruction of the Negro community there. I know that advocates of violence in that community are urging their people to strike first. I know this will explode into a bloody war in the streets, at any minute, unless I can persuade you to help.

"Black Power is not threatening this city. It is being threatened by a criminal group who have cleverly pointed away from themselves, placing the blame on an already outraged segment of our population. You have got to stop, and listen, and think. If you light the fuse that destroys this city and results in the butchering of thousands of people, you'll have to share that guilt for the rest of your lives. Oh, you may watch it safely on your television sets for the moment. But eventually you will have to go out onto the streets for the simple necessities of food and drink. There you will find anarchy, shops smashed and looted, and murderous hatred in the eyes of the stranger you meet face to face on the pavement.

"Your life is at stake if this violence begins.

"The mayor of this city is a brave man. He will not order the police or the Army to move first. Trained detectives, members of the District Attorney's staff, FBI agents, and experienced newsmen are working around the clock to expose the real blackmailers of this city. They ask for time, they ask for calm, they ask for what our young people today call 'cool.' You can only destroy yourselves by striking out blindly, with bigotry and hatred.

"I tell you again, Black Power is not at the root of this danger. Don't be persuaded that it is. Don't let the demagogues turn you into the murderers of thousands of innocent people. What happens in this city in the next twenty-nine hours can never be undone.

"This last I direct to one man, John Sprague. Listen to me, Sprague. Early last evening you convinced me that Black Power was not involved in blackmailing this city. I believed you. I still believe you. I have put my personal integrity on the block for you. Listen to me. The army will not come to Harlem. The mobs will not be allowed to reach you. I can't guarantee there won't be an isolated skirmish here and there on the outskirts. Things may have gone too far to prevent that. But the power that can steamroller your people to death will not be turned loose—*unless you start it!* We're fighting to get at the truth, John Sprague. Give us the time."

"If I have reached any of you at all, you are asking 'What can I do?' Turn back from whatever thoughts of violence you have; turn your neighbor back. Give the Mayor and his officials a chance to deal with the real criminals instead of fighting their own people.

"We are confronted by a cold-blooded, cunningly planned crime, not a race war. Don't turn it into one. If you do, you may not live to regret it!"

The red light blinked off on the camera. Peter leaned back in his chair, drenched with sweat. Potter came out of the control booth.

"Nice going, Mr. Styles. Right on the button. Four-twenty-nine."

Peter glanced up at the TV monitor. A girl was dangling her bare feet in a brook, smoking a menthol cigarette.

"I should have added, this 'may be hazardous to your health,' " Peter said.

A voice came over the intercom from the booth.

"Mr. Styles wanted on the telephone."

Peter headed for the booth. Marshall was on the other end. "Finished?"

"Just."

"Severance has had the word."

"The word?"

"How to deliver the money," Marshall said. "The Mayor has set up a temporary headquarters in the Roosevelt. Come on down and we'll go over." . . .

The first thing Peter asked Marshall as he walked into the station master's office was: "Have you heard from Grace?"

"My dear fellow, she's hardly had time to get there. Let's go. We can get into the Roosevelt from the station."

"These surrounding hotels aren't the safest places in town, are they?"

"It's not Ramsay's idea to present an image of safety for city officials," Marshall said. "The hotels are a problem. Thousands of guests. How to get them to leave? The Roosevelt, the Biltmore, and the Commodore all have exits directly into the station."

They walked through the deserted station, accompanied by McComas. The emptiness was eerie.

"Severance got a phone call?" Peter asked.

Marshall nodded. "It's a crazy situation," he said. "You asked a good question earlier. Why haven't the calls been monitored? They just don't come if Severance is covered in any way. Only the first call came to his home. One later to his office. We've had him tailed so that, wherever he was, he could signal us when a call came through. No calls. They seem to be watching him through a magnifying glass. We've finally pulled off all surveillance, and the Mayor has him constantly moving around town, giving them the opportunity to reach him when they want to. We can't risk their not being able to contact him as the time closes in on us. He's on his way to the Roosevelt now. I don't know yet where the call reached him."

They climbed a flight of stone stairs and up into the lobby of the hotel. Two policemen guarded the entrance—which was also an exit. The Mayor had occupied a suite on the fourth floor. An elevator whisked them up. Two plainclothes men were stationed outside the suite's door.

The Honorable James Ramsay sat at an improvised conference table. Most of his Ivy League slickness was gone.

He was coatless and tieless. An electric razor on the table beside him indicated he was managing his toilet on the run. There was a haggard look in his ordinarily bright eyes. There was a telephone at his elbow, and Peter could hear someone talking on another phone in the adjoining room.

"Thank you for coming, gentlemen," he said. He gestured toward a TV set in the corner. "They've just run your tape, Mr. Styles. I want to thank you. It's very good. Let's hope to God that people have ears to listen."

"Any news from Harlem?" Peter asked.

"Huge crowds milling around," Ramsay said. "John Sprague touring on a sound truck, whipping people into a frenzy. My men up there say they could break loose any minute. If they do, God help us. I understand your friend, Mrs. Minafee, is trying to get to Sprague to reason with him. Do you think there's any chance he'll listen?"

"He's been looking for a chance like this to seize power—he and his counterparts—like for a hundred years," Peter said. "That's our problem, Mr. Mayor. We face a crisis that developed three weeks ago. They face one that's been building since their great-grandparents were brought here from Africa in chains. That stew has been boiling for a very long time. I wonder if we can cool it with a television speech, or the persuasive arguments of one attractive woman."

"Sprague has got to see the facts!" Ramsay said, his voice hoarse with fatigue. "If he forces us to, we can wipe him and all his people out. We'll have no choice. We can be his protectors or his assassins. The choice is his."

"If I were Sprague," Peter said, "I'd be weighing a number of possibilities. He's not just a bloodthirsty lunatic, Mr. Mayor. He's a violent crusader for what he believes to be a just cause; the endless frustration and degradation of his people. Suppose he accepts your offer of protection and cools off his followers? He'll be exactly where he was before this all happened; perhaps not so well off. There are millions of people who heard the first accusation—that Black Power is threatening the city—and they'll never hear anything else no matter how often we tell them. There will be new laws passed in the State Legislature and the Congress, adding new repressions and restrictions. New chains. That's inevitable, Mr. Mayor, and you know it."

Ramsay nodded, wearily, his hands raised to his face.

"So what is his alternative? He has his people whipped to a fever pitch. He can send them out into the streets with guns, and clubs, and Molotov cocktails. They will be heard, Mr. Mayor. My God, they will be heard."

"And they will be mowed down by the military."

"Yes, they will die, most of them. And the whole country will look at our gutters running with blood, and there is a good chance that the revulsion will be so great that at last the Negro cause will have a receptive audience. That may be what Sprague sees. The Christian martyrs were slaughtered by the Roman emperors, but Christianity survived. Sprague may see his own death and the massacre of thousands of his people as the one way to assure a permanent hearing."

"God forbid," Ramsay said.

The door to the suite opened and Martin Severance came in. He was in sharp contrast to the rest of them, cool and refreshed. He nodded curtly to Peter and Marshall and stood facing the Mayor across the table.

"Well, let's have it, Martin," Ramsay said.

"I was buying cigarettes at the newsstand near my apartment building," Severance said. "The call came there— pay phone booth."

"They must be right on your heels," Marshall said.

Severance nodded. "I sometimes have the feeling they're breathing on my neck!"

"And this time?"

"The mechanics of paying the ransom," Severance said. He shook his head. "It seems, God help me, that I am to be the go-between; the paymaster."

"And the mechanics?"

"The money, as we have already been told, is to be in unmarked bills in denominations of no more than a hundred dollars. The money is to be given to me to deliver."

"You'll need a truck to carry it!" Marshall said.

"Trunk of my car," Severance said. "I am to be ready to deliver it at high noon tomorrow. If I'm not, there will be no further contact, and they will carry out their plan, whether the station is closed or open.'

"And where do you deliver it?" Marshall asked.

"I'm to head up the East River Drive, across the Triboro Bridge and onto the Major Deegan thruway. If I'm not followed, I will be contacted. If I am—and this includes helicopter observation—I can drive until I run out of gas and that will be that."

"Any other specifics?" Marshall asked.

"I have two cars—a sports car and a regular sedan. I am to drive the sedan, a grey Buick."

"So let's take a guess," Marshall said. "If you are contacted, you will be told to stop at a gas station. At that gas station will be another grey Buick sedan, a duplicate of yours. You will get out to pay for gas, and you will get into the other car and drive off. When you're out of sight someone will take your car—and the money."

"The Major Deegan could be covered from one end to the

other," Ramsay said.

"The gas station won't be on the Deegan," Marshall said. "It'll be on some side street in the Bronx or in Yonkers or some other off-area."

"We could provide Martin with a two-way radio for his car," Ramsay said.

"If they know where he buys cigarettes, do you suppose his car isn't being watched?" Marshall asked. He shook his head. "If you're going to pay the ransom, Jim, you'd better not try to get tricky in the process."

"I would have to leave my apartment house garage about eleven in the morning," Severance said. "That would give me just an hour to make contact. Have you made up your mind, Jim—whether to pay or not?"

Ramsay hesitated. Peter guessed what he was thinking. There were no secrets. Suddenly the harrassed Mayor didn't trust any of them.

"Be ready, Martin," Ramsay said. "We'll arrange to get the money to you and packed in your car. My decision will come at eleven o'clock tomorrow morning; your starting time."

"Fair enough," Severance said.

"It's like a bad dream," Ramsay said to himself.

3

There was no message from Grace, when Peter and Marshall got back to the station master's office. O'Connor, the Police Commissioner, had gloomy news of Harlem.

"We've got dozens of Negro plainclothes men mingling with the crowds up there," he said. "They say Sprague sounds like Hitler addressing one of his beer hall rallies—the crowd reacting the same way. They say there's going to be no checking him. When he gets them steamed up to just the right pitch, he'll give the word—and that's that. I think the Mayor ought to put General Danvers on a stand-by."

"If I know the General, he's straining at the leash," Marshall said.

"I'm going up there," Peter said.

"Don't be a damn fool, Peter."

"You sent Grace up there. I'm going after her. God knows what will happen to her if she tries to force her way to Sprague."

"I'll send you in a squad car with a couple of men," Marshall said. He knew better than to argue.

"I advise against that, Jerry," O'Connor said. "A squad car and cops trying to wedge their way into that mob might be just the thing to pull the trigger."

"Take me as close as it makes sense," Peter said. "I'll make the rest of it on my own."

"You're not going to be welcome," O'Connor said.

"They came to me last night. I'm going to them today," Peter said.

There were strange sights on the way uptown. There were masses of troops at the north end of Central Park, not fifteen blocks from the edge of trouble. The north-and-south streets were blocked off, with machine guns behind barricades of trucks.

"They're asking for it!" Peter said.

His patrolman-driver nodded. "The Mayor drew a line across One hundred tenth Street," he said. "Troops are not to go above it; mobs are not to come below it. In between here and One hundred twenty-fifth Street is no-man's land."

"I better walk it from here," Peter said.

The cop looked at him. "You have to be a hero or out of your cotton-picking mind," he said.

"If your girl was up there would you go after her?"

"You know it," the cop said.

"That's how it is," Peter said.

He got out of the squad car. The pavement felt hot under his feet. He walked north. The quiet of yesterday still existed here; no children on the streets, no one on the fire-escapes. No one! But to the north there was a noise like the sound of a giant cheering section at a football game.

He walked rapidly, sweat running down inside his clothes. The words of the chant presently became clear to him.

"Kill! Kill! Kill!"

He moistened his lips and broke into a running jog. There began to be people now in windows, looking north. They were black people. Somebody jeered at him. A milk carton dropped just in front of him from a height and spattered his trouser legs with white.

He was within a block of the roaring crowd, when someone reached out of an alley and grabbed his arm. He tried to wrench free, and then, as he swung around he recognized the man as the giant Negro who had been Nathan Jones' sentinel the morning before.

"Got word you were coming," the man said. "The boss wants to see you."

"Let go of my arm," Peter said.

"After I tell you if you go another block you may get yourself killed," the man said. He let go of Peter's arm.

"Where's Jones?" Peter asked.

"Next building, top floor," the man said. "You can see the whole circus from there. Come peaceful, huh? Nathan may be able to help you."

He needed help. He followed the Negro down a filth-crowded alley, cut behind another alley and through a cellar way. They climbed stairs, endless stairs. There was a stifling odor of onions and cabbage and cooking fat and sour toilets. Finally the Negro knocked on a door—a short-long-short signal-type knock. Somebody slid a bolt on the inside and the door opened. A pretty Negro girl stood aside to let them in. Across the room, at the front windows, Peter saw Nathan Jones looking out.

"So Eddie found you," Jones said, without turning. "You ever watch a volcano erupt? You may get a chance."

Through the open window came the sound of a voice

bellowing over a loud speaker. And then the chant.

"Kill! Kill! Kill!"

Peter reached the window. There was a clear view of One hundred Twenty-fifth Street, packed from wall to wall with people. In the center of the mass, a man stood on a flat-bodied truck with multiple loud speakers surrounding him. Peter recognized the giant body, the orange sports shirt, the blue baseball cap.

"We've asked for all these years!" Sprague shouted. "We've begged on our knees for all these years. Now we're gonna take!"

"Kill! Kill! Kill!" the crowd roared.

"The day of slavery is over! We win our freedom with our blood!"

"Kill! Kill! Kill!"

"Quite a spellbinder, our Johnny," Jones said. He glanced at his watch. "He's got a little while to waste before he gives the signal. Would you believe it if I told you they've got a boat in the East River with guns on it? They're going to shell the United Nations building." For the first time he turned to look at Peter through the opaque black glasses. "You must be a congenital idiot to send Mrs. Minafee up here, Styles."

"Where is she?"

"I wish I could tell you," Jones said. "She was suddenly in the crowd out there. A lot of those people are her friends, but not today. Not today, man. They half tore the clothes off her and they bounced her around. But somehow, by God, she managed to get to the truck, shouting at Johnny. When he saw her he had her dragged up onto the truck. He talked to her a minute, and then he swung her around by the arm, like he was about to auction her off. 'Our friend, Mrs. Minafee, has come to us with the same old baloney,' he told the crowd.

163

'Wait, and give 'em a chance to get readier for us! Wait, and give 'em a chance to bring in more troops, and more guns, and more gas! What shall we tell her?' Well, you know the answer, Styles. 'Kill! Kill! Kill!' So they dragged her down off the truck, and that's the last I saw of her."

Peter was shaking. "And you just sat here?"

"And I just sat here," Jones said. "I'm not welcome down there. I believe in peaceful means, remember? But I'm the one who'll write the truth about what happens, if there are any black men left alive to read it."

"I've got to find Grace," Peter said.

"Down there?" Jones laughed bitterly. "Man, you can't walk twenty feet down there. The blood lust is running high, Styles. They'd take delight in practicing on you."

"Do you have any idea where she could be? Where they could have taken her?"

"I just sat here," Jones said, "but I do have a couple of boys nosing around. You wait—and watch the fun."

"She came here to help," Peter said. "We've had instructions for the payoff. We've got a day, Nathan. We need it. Those people down there need it, because if they follow Sprague they've had it. The Army is entrenched not fifteen blocks from here."

"They know that," Jones said. "They know it and it doesn't matter. 'Into the valley of death rode the six hundred.' "

"It's mass suicide."

"But maybe some of their kids will live. They're not living now."

Peter's mouth felt dry. His throat muscles ached. Looking down at that seething mass of hysterical people he forgot about a war in the streets, about a bomb threat, about anything except the hopelessness of trying to find Grace. He turned to Jones. His lips moved, but words wouldn't come out. There was the faintest narrowing of sympathy at the corners of Jones' eyes, hidden by the black glasses.

"I wouldn't kid you, man," Jones said. "I don't know where she is." He turned back to look down at the street. The kill chant rose loud and insistent. "I sometimes think man was never made to be a communal animal," he said. "When they get together in crowds, they go crazy. But when it hits home, personally, they forget all about causes, and the greatest good for the greatest number, and they just think about what's going to happen to ME. The only thing that matters is ME. That's where you are right now, Styles. All that matters to you is Mrs. Minafee."

"You're a mind reader," Peter whispered. He looked out over the expanse of black, dirty roofs. She was out there, perhaps in one of those buildings, perhaps crumpled in an alley. He felt the impulse to shout out his agony and frustration at the top of his lungs.

The sharp signal-knock came at the door of the tiny apartment. The Negro girl appeared from a back room and slid open the bolt. The door opened.

Standing outside was a Negro in a bright cerise sports shirt. He wore the black glasses that seemed to be almost a part of a uniform. He had a thin mustache and a small goatee. Peter recognized him as one of the men who'd been at his apartment with Sprague the night before. The man's mouth was a thin, hostile slit.

Suddenly all of Peter's anxiety and pent-up fury seemed to focus on this man.

"What have you done with Mrs. Minafee?" he asked, in a voice that shook under the effort at control.

"She deserves worse than she got," the man said.

Peter launched himself forward. The man took a quick side step inside the door, and a switchblade knife glittered in the sunlight from the windows. "Don't tempt me, man," he said.

"Take it easy," Nathan Jones said, sharply. He put a restraining hand on Peter's arm. "This is Ricky Knowles, one of Johnny's boys."

"We've met," Peter said.

"You don't have the sense God gave a newborn baby—you and your Mrs. Minafee," Knowles said. "You need a diagram drawn to see we aren't throwing a party for white cats out there?" He nodded toward the window.

"What about Mrs. Minafee?" Peter said, doggedly. He was looking at Knowles through a red haze.

"You want to see her, I'll take you to her," Knowles said. "Johnny wants to talk to you."

"Now," Peter said.

Knowles shrugged. "You, too, Nathan," he said. "Johnny wants a witness."

"Where to?" Jones asked.

"Power plant," Knowles said.

They went down the flights of stairs to the basement level, through the fog of cooking odors, and out into the back alley. Knowles led the way, not looking back once.

"There's a laundry about three blocks away," Jones said at Peter's elbow. "They got a generating system where they make their own power."

The alleys behind the miserable tenement buildings were knee deep in filth. Rats perched on back steps, glaring at them belligerently. They finally reached the rear of a square brick building, and Knowles opened a metal fire door and went in.

A roar of sound greeted Peter. Half a dozen big generators were operating full blast. The vibration shook the building from stem to stern. Knowles had started up an iron stairway. Peter followed with Nathan Jones bringing up the rear. They climbed to what Peter guessed was a fourth floor level, high over the noisy generators. There was a small, glassed-in office, at the far end of an iron catwalk. Just before they reached the door, Knowles stopped and turned to Peter. He pointed down over the iron handrail. Peter froze, his hands gripping the rail. Far down, in what looked like a small machine shop, he saw Grace. She was sitting on the floor. Her dress had been torn off one bronzed shoulder. Her head was lowered and her face was covered with her hands.

"Grace!" Peter shouted at the top of his lungs.

The huge generators threw back a thunder of sardonic sound. Grace didn't move. She couldn't have heard him if he'd been able to shout ten times louder. He turned back toward the iron stairs. Knowles spun him around.

"You want to give her a chance, you better talk to Johnny!" he shouted. He gestured toward the frosted glass door of the little office.

Peter looked down at Grace again. He waved his arms in futile windmill gestures. She didn't look up. She had no reason to look up.

Knowles was tugging at Peter. Reluctantly Peter turned and followed through the door and into the office. The sound was shut out to a large extent in the bare office, but the whole place shook and trembled. Johnny Sprague, his orange sport shirt black with sweat, was perched on the edge of a flat-topped desk, his head tilted back, drinking a bottle of soft drink in one long swallow. He slammed the empty bottle down on the table and looked at Peter through his heavy black glasses.

"Don't waste your breath, Styles, telling me what a son-ofabitch I am," he said. "I had your Mrs. Minafee dragged off the sound truck out there and brought here. If I hadn't, she'd have been stomped to death. She got pushed around some, but she's all in one piece."

"How do I get her out of here?" Peter asked.

"That's why I had Ricky bring you," Sprague said. "To tell you how. I wouldn't be here at all if I didn't have troubles of my own." His huge fist came down hard on the desk top. "You don't keep gasoline around where kids are fooling with matches," he said. Even in this little office the noise was enough to make loud talking necessary. It made Sprague sound even angrier. "We've been gathering a supply of guns and small arms for a long time. Didn't keep 'em in the neighborhood. Too many cats ready to start something on their own—like Ricky, here. We had 'em stored in an old warehouse up in Yonkers. Well, today was to be the day. A couple of hours ago I sent two trucks up to Yonkers to bring back the guns, so we could pass 'em out. The trucks haven't come back. You know why? This crazy General Calhoun and his racist army have hi-jacked 'em. They're sitting up in Van Cortlandt Park, hundreds of 'em, waiting for Calhoun to give the order for them to turn our guns on us! We're caught in a nutcracker. Army below us, Calhoun above us. So after all I've got to call it off, and there's only one way."

"If you don't turn Mrs. Minafee over to me—," Peter began, as if he hadn't heard.

"To hell with Mrs. Minafee!" Sprague shouted. "You listen to me, white boy, or I turn your Mrs. Minafee over to the sharks. There's thousands of 'em out there on the street, and they're woman eaters!" He leaned forward. "We've got one chance; one stinkin' miserable chance. Drag the real villain of this situation in front of the television cameras with a confession; HE wrote the note, HE threatened the city. Then the Mayor will call off the Army, and Calhoun won't dare move because the public reaction would be too hot for him to handle."

"I'll be as honest with you as you have been with me," Peter said. "We haven't got even a shadow of a lead."

"I know you haven't," Sprague said. "But I have. So you listen. There's a marina up here on the East River—a boat yard. They repair small yachts and power boats for the rich cats who live up in the Riverdale section. Some of our people work there, caulking, painting. They finished repairs on a yacht there last week. Belonged to a fellow named Roger Mansfield. Mansfield paid for the job by check and took his boat away. Like fifty-five hundred bucks. The check bounced."

Peter waited, puzzled. "So?" he said.

"This Mansfield is an ex-Navy officer," Sprague said. "Ordinance. He was a demolition expert. He knows all about big-time explosions—all stuff like that. He would know how to make a bomb."

"But how do you connect him with all this? There are thousands of men who know how to make a bomb."

"His check bounced. He needs money," Sprague said.

Find a man who needs ten million dollars, G. Bailey Thoms had advised. "But there's still nothing to connect Mansfield to the threat," Peter said.

The corner of Sprague's mouth twitched. "Martin Severance is Mansfield's brother-in-law," he said. "That's the message."

Peter felt a sudden cold chill run along his spine. Severance!

"I got chewin' on this, man," Sprague said. "Severance is the only one who's had any contact with the blackmailers. They phoned him—he says! They wrote him a letter—he says!"

"He's just gotten word on how to deliver the ransom money," Peter said.

"*He* says!"

It was wild. It wasn't believable. But it could be. Severance! Severance, smooth and cool; Severance, the Mayor's friend and confidant; Severance, the only contact with—Severance? Severance, whose brother-in-law is an explosives expert. Severance, with ten million dollars in the trunk of his car which he will take to—Severance?

"You can imagine what would happen if one of us was to try to convince the Honorable James Ramsay that his buddy is back of this," Sprague said.

Sprague was right, Peter knew. No one would listen to Sprague, a dangerous fanatic. He could imagine what would happen if he presented the notion to Ramsay himself. He'd be laughed out of court. He could visualize Severance listening to the suggestion without batting an eyelid. "You should write fiction, Mr. Styles."

"You're not laughing," Sprague said. "That's why I give it to you, man. You'll give it a run for its money, right?"

Nathan Jones was looking at Peter. "You'll be known from here on in as the idiot child, Styles. But, by God, it could be!"

"Turn Mrs. Minafee over to me and I'll do what I can," Peter said.

"Not on your life!" Sprague shouted. "I got to be sure of you, man. I got to be sure you want this as bad as I do!"

Peter's mouth tightened. "How much time do I have?"

"God only knows how soon those lunatics in the parks will start shooting," Sprague said. "That's how long you got. When that happens, we start fighting machine guns with broken bottles. When that happens, I couldn't get your Mrs. Minafee out of here if I went down on my knees and begged."

"How do I get out of here?" Peter asked, his voice grim.

"Ricky will take you."

"Can Mrs. Minafee be told that I'm trying?"

Sprague shrugged. "Why not? Deep down we know you haven't got a chance, man. There's no one will listen to you—not in time." . . .

Peter got another look at Grace as Knowles led him out into the inferno of sound and down the iron stairway. There was no way to attract her attention. She was leaning back against the wall now, her eyes closed. God, if she'd just open them and look up. The noise must be driving her out of her mind.

Knowles led Peter out through the maze of alleys again to a side street. A Negro taxi-driver waited there, obviously by pre-arrangement. Peter asked to be driven as close to Grand Central as the police would allow.

There was one person who wouldn't laugh, Peter knew; Jerry Marshall, the District Attorney, would listen, and wonder, and help.

Forty-seventh Street was as close as the taxi was allowed to get to Grand Central. It was only when Peter started to pay the driver that he realized the flag hadn't been thrown.

"On the house," the driver said, grinning. "I, for one, hope you get lucky, Mr. Styles."

Peter realized he had no way of getting back into the station; no pass, no credentials. He went into a drugstore and called the station master's office. Marshall told him to come through the Roosevelt and McComas would be waiting at the blocked-off entrance to the station.

The crowd noises weren't as sharp down here; just a steady angry hum. McComas was waiting at the appointed place.

"Any luck?"

"Maybe. Just maybe."

They walked hurriedly through the hollow tunnel to the station master's office. The place was crowded now. In addition to Marshall, O'Connor and Mayberry, there were a dozen experts of one sort or another, huddled in a perpetual buzz of conversation. Peter distracted Marshall from one of these huddles, a hand on his arm.

"Mrs. Minafee?" Marshall asked.

"Safe—for now. I need you privately and in a hurry," Peter said.

Marshall took him through a door at the end of the room. It was a space for filing, with only narrow aisles between rows and rows of green metal cabinets. No place to sit down.

"You're going to need to hold onto your hat," Peter said. He told the story as it had come to him from Sprague, with no conclusions drawn. A man had a yacht repaired, he paid for it by check, the check bounced. This man is an ex-Navy officer, a demolition expert with special knowledge of high explosives. This man, Roger Mansfield, is Martin Severance's brother-in-law.

Marshall's bloodshot eyes stared at him. "That's all?"

"That's all."

Marshall's breath made a whistling noise between his teeth.

"Who received the threat? Severance," he said, softly. "Proof? His word. Who received the letter? Severance. Proof that he actually received it and didn't manufacture it himself? His word. Who has received all the other calls, including the last one which is supposed to have told him how to deliver the money? Severance. Proof? His word."

"Thanks for not laughing," Peter said.

"I ought to have my head examined," Marshall said. "I'm going to tell you something, Peter, that even the Mayor doesn't know. My office has been investigating rumors of special influence in the awarding of city contracts. All the city commissioners who have the right to award contracts have been under my office microscope. Severance is one of them. No special finger was pointed at him, you understand. But he was an important one because he hands out some pretty large construction contracts. Right on my desk are facts about him I should have related to this. His personal finances are in bad shape. He owes a hell of a lot of money. Oh, he could probably pay up if he was pressed. His wife is loaded. He has that cooperative apartment on Beekman Place and a summer home in Westchester. He could pay up if he liquidated his assets, but he'd be stripped pretty clean. It had me looking for kickbacks on these contracts he awards."

"And he was getting them?"

"Not a shred of proof. But he needs money, Peter. He needs money badly. That I can prove, but it doesn't connect him with this. It could take months of digging." Marshall jerked his head up. "How much time does Sprague give us?"

"Not long. Not much time at all." He explained that Calhoun's Army for a Basic America was ready to strike.

"You've thought of the note? That typewritten note from 'Black Power'?" Marshall asked.

"What about it?"

"An expert could match up the right typewriter with the threat letter in two minutes," Marshall said. "But we'll have to have samples from the machines Severance might have used. I can have samples from the machines in his office in fifteen minutes. I'll have a detective go in as a maintenance man, check all machines. But I doubt like hell Severance would have used an office machine."

"Does he have one at home?"

"Everybody owns a portable typewriter these days. He's probably got one in his apartment and another one in the country. They're more difficult to get at. You don't just walk into a man's home and check his typewriter. It's not like the gas company or the electric company."

"Court order?" Peter asked.

"Could take hours unless I could lay hands on just the right judge," Marshall said. "Severance is a political figure, the Mayor's close friend. I'd have to build a hell of a good case. I haven't got one. And we haven't got time."

"Is Severance apt to be at his apartment?" Peter asked.

"In and out. He's supposed to stay in touch. That's where we're to reach him."

"Suppose I went to see him," Peter said. "He knows I'm on the inside. I could bluff something about a lead I got in Harlem—something that would justify my asking him some questions about the telephone voice. When I got through, I could ask to borrow his typewriter to work on my notes. There's no way he can suspect we're on to him."

"It's worth a try," Marshall said.

"Suppose the typewriter he used is in the country?"

"I like the idea that it's the one in the apartment," Marshall said. "It was a secret sort of thing. He had to compose the ransom note so it would sound like it came from the place he wanted us to believe it came from. He'd want to be alone. That's why I doubt we'll come up with an office machine that matches. In the country there's his wife and three or four servants. I buy the apartment. He spends a lot of time there. Shall I phone him you're coming?"

"I think not," Peter said. "I think I'd prefer to walk in on him."

"You've got to play it awfully cool," Marshall said. "Don't let yourself be hurried or he may smell the hook."

"It's not going to be easy," Peter said. "I feel like murdering the sonofabitch in cold blood."

Marshall's eyes narrowed. "Just remember, Peter, he may be completely innocent. This is a long, long guess from way out! While you're at it, I'll have his office covered and the results checked. When you get a sample from his machine, bring it here as fast as you can. I'll have the expert here ready to give us an answer."

"Pray for me—and for Grace," Peter said. . . .

The city was enveloped in a hot haze. It seemed as if the gods had arranged the day to match the smouldering hatreds that stalked the streets.

There were no taxis in the station area at all. Rather than wait and hope, Peter headed up town on foot. The Beekman Place apartment Severance owned was in the fifties. The building looked down on the river, and to the right was the rectangular tower that was the United Nations building.

There should have been an attendant in the lobby, but there was no one. Peter guessed that a lot of posts like this had been deserted. People were curious about where the action was. The man who should have been here in the lobby may have had a family in the danger area.

There was a little directory board over the desk where the attendant should have been. MARTIN SEVERANCE, 901. The elevator was set on self-service. Peter stepped in and pressed the 9 button. The door was noiseless. The rise was almost without sensation. Nine-o-one was on the river side, at the far end of the hall. Peter tried to get the cotton-dry feel out of his mouth before he pressed the doorbell. He could hear a chime, like a ship's bell, on the inside.

The door opened and Peter was faced by a stranger.

The stranger was a big man, broad shouldered, wearing grey flannel slacks and a blue yachting blazer with brass buttons and a club patch over the breast pocket. An Ivy League sportsman, Peter thought.

"Is Mr. Severance in?"

"Out for a few minutes," the man said, pleasantly.

"My name is Peter Styles. I'm anxious to find him."

"Styles! The *Newsview* guy. You're in on this tea party, aren't you? Martin's out walking around. Part of his job. In case they want to phone him, you know. I'm Martin's brother-in-law, Roger Mansfield."

The handshake was a crusher.

"Come on in and wait," Mansfield said.

Like a man walking on eggs, Peter stepped past Mansfield into the apartment's living room. It was furnished in exquisite early American. Peter recognized Wyeth and Benton paintings on the wall. He wondered if the taste belonged to the coolly aloof Severance or perhaps to his wife.

Mansfield was hearty. "Anything new cooking?" he asked.

"I've just come back from Harlem. The temperature there is high."

"Black bastards," Mansfield said. "Could I get you something? Coffee? We drink it by the gallons here, just sitting around and waiting. Too early in the day for a drink?"

Peter struggled to keep his voice casual. "Coffee would be fine," he said. "By the way, do you happen to have a typewriter here? I made a lot of scribbled notes while I was uptown. While I'm waiting for Severance it would help if I could type them up."

"Help yourself," Mansfield said. "There's a portable on Martin's desk in the study through that door."

"Thanks," Peter said. There was a chance he could get a sample of the machine's typing without having to face Severance at all.

The study was a small room, intended originally to be a bedroom. The portable, protected by a plastic cover, rested on a small square table. There was no indication that Severance carried on any very heavy business here. The table was bare. Peter sat down behind the machine and lifted off the cover. In the center drawer of the table he found some sheets of Severance's personal note paper. He rolled a page into the machine and began to type quickly. It was necessary to get every letter and number and punctuation mark and symbol onto the paper.

He heard Mansfield's heavy footsteps.

"Forgot to ask you what you take in your coffee," the big man said from the door.

"As it comes."

"Be hot in a second," Mansfield said, and withdrew.

Peter's fingers flew over the keyboard. Then he heard the sound of a door opening and closing.

"Roger?" Severance called out.

"You got a visitor," Peter heard Mansfield call out. "Styles. He's in your study."

Peter rolled the paper out of the machine and began to stuff it into his jacket pocket. Severance was in the doorway, his black eyes cold and hostile.

"Been writing up some notes while I waited for you," Peter said. He recovered the portable and stood up. "Thanks for the use of your machine."

Mansfield appeared beside his brother-in-law, holding a cup of coffee.

"My typewriters seem to be interesting to a lot of people," Severance said, his voice tight and hard. "I just talked to my secretary at the office. There's a maintenance man there now, checking the machines. It seems rather odd, since there was a man there only yesterday who put them all in order." He turned to the big man in the yachtsman's blazer and exploded. "You stupid sonofabitch!" he said.

"What's wrong, Marty?" Mansfield sounded stunned.

Severance ignored him. "Can I have a look at your notes, Styles?"

"Not much point," Peter said.

"You were just trying to get a sample of the machine's typing. Right?"

"Yes, I'm afraid that's right," Peter said.

"I don't get it, Marty," Mansfield said.

"You just lost yourself a couple of million bucks," Severance said, without looking at him.

"You mean—"

"Yes, I mean," Severance said. He took a cigarette out of the pocket of his beautifully tailored suit and lit it. His hands were quite steady. The cold, handsome face looked chiseled out of stone.

178

"How did you get onto it?" he asked.

"A bad check," Peter said. "The relationship between you and Mansfield. Two and two."

"That thing in your pocket will match the ransom letter," Severance said, totally controlled.

"I assumed it would."

"Who else knows?"

"Jerry Marshall."

"That accounts for the phony maintenance man in my office."

"Yes." Peter drew a deep breath. "So the game is up, Severance. You could make things go easier for you."

"How?"

"A quick public confession that will stop this city from being ripped apart by riots."

Severance's expression didn't change by a hair. "How much?" he asked. "I can get you another typing sample in a very few minutes. Half a million dollars make it worth your while?"

"No," Peter said.

"It's negotiable," Severance said.

"Sorry."

The coffee cup rattled in Mansfield's hands. He put it down on a table inside the door. "You're not so very bright yourself, Marty," he said, in an unsteady voice. "Why the hell didn't you get rid of that typewriter?"

"Angela gave it to me. She'd have asked questions," Severance said. "My wife is a question asker, Styles. I didn't think we had a problem."

"You just going to let him walk out of here and turn us in?" Mansfield asked.

"You have to be kidding," Severance said.

"You don't have much choice," Peter said. "Marshall knows I'm here. If I don't get back to him pretty quickly—"

"He'll come here looking for you," Severance said. "You will not be here. Nor will the typewriter, by the way. Something must have happened to you on the way here. The streets are full of uncontrolled people today." He spoke to Mansfield without turning his head. "Will he fit into the trunk of the sports car?"

"We'll make him fit," Mansfield said.

"You don't think, guessing what they do, that Marshall will let the Mayor turn you loose tomorrow morning with all that cash in your car?"

"You're forcing me to play the game move by move," Severance said. "You are problem number one, Styles. My garage is in the basement of this building. We will take you and the typewriter to Roger's boat and dump the load somewhere appropriately far out at sea. Let's go, Roger."

Severance and Mansfield moved into the room. It left almost no space to maneuver

"This is going to hurt me worse than it will you," Mansfield said, with a kind of idiot grin. "Too bad a nice guy like you couldn't be sensible."

An absurd memory flashed across Peter's mind screen. It was the voice of the commando drill sergeant in Korea. "Kick to the kneecap, which freezes the leg; back kick to the shin, which breaks the leg; edge of the hand to the windpipe, which shatters the larynx box; chop to the back of the neck as he falls forward, which breaks the neck as he goes down."

Mansfield was on him, his great powerful hands closing on Peter's throat. In that moment Peter knew that only some miracle stood between him and death. He brought up his knee with all the strength he had to Mansfield's groin. He heard the scream of pain as he staggered back, his artificial leg failing to give him the proper balance he needed.

Severance, his face showing no more emotion than it had during one of the Mayor's conferences, had picked up a brass-handled poker from a set of fireplace tools in the corner. He swung it from side to side, like a man cracking a whip. Peter ducked under the first murderous swish and managed to get hold of the straight-backed maple desk chair in which he had been sitting. He held it up as a shield and it broke like matchwood in his hands as Severance swung again. Peter braced his good leg against the wall and projected himself forward in a low, hard dive at Severance's ankles—a football tackle. He had to get into close quarters if his brains weren't to be spattered on the wall by that swinging bar of iron.

Severance went down very hard. Peter, twisting loose, saw the doorway cleared for a moment. He struggled up, kicked with his metal foot at Severance's face, and lurched toward the door. There was a roar of anger behind him as he staggered into the living room. Mansfield had recovered enough to rejoin the attack. He must literally have hurled himself through space to land on Peter's back. Peter went down under two hundred and forty pounds of bone and muscle.

"I got him, Marty!" Mansfield shouted. "Bring that poker in here!"

A powerful arm went around Peter's neck, pulling his head back and up. He screamed, for the simple comfort of hearing his own voice for the last time. He could hear Severance scrambling in from the study.

And then the apartment seemed to explode. It sounded, absurdly to Peter, like machine-gun fire. There was a sound of splintering wood. The torturing arm around Peter's neck loosened. With the last ounce of energy he had Peter rolled and twisted away from the weight that attempted to pin him down.

"Hold it right where you are, dad!" a voice shouted.

The room was full of voices, oddly familiar voices. Someone screamed.

"Break both his arms if you want, Ricky, but don't hit him in the mouth," Johnny Sprague's voice said. "He's got to be able to talk."

Peter managed to get to his hands and knees. He looked through a fog of pain at the scene. Sprague was holding a Tommy gun on a gaping Mansfield. Ricky Knowles had Severance's right arm twisted behind him, holding him up by it, as Severance's knees buckled under him. Saliva ran out of the corner of his agonized mouth.

"Took you a long time to make any noise, man," Sprague said to Peter. "We couldn't figure out what was happening till you yelled. Where do we get Severance to a television camera? General Calhoun is making a speech up north." . . .

Mayor Ramsay and Martin Severance and Sprague faced the cameras in the television studio in Grand Central Station. Behind the glass in the control booth, Peter, Jerry Marshall, Ricky Knowles and a dozen officials watched. Mansfield had been carted off to a nearby precinct station house. The Mayor made a statement, and then Severance, clutching at his left arm which hung crooked and useless at his side, began a halting confession.

"I conceived the idea—I wrote the letter which supposedly

182

confirmed the phone calls I never really got—my brother-in-law manufactured the bomb which was found in the Commodore—he had access to—" The voice went on and on.

Peter looked at Ricky Knowles. "How in the name of God did you happen to get to that apartment?" he asked.

Knowles shrugged. "I wasn't for it. But Nathan convinced Johnny. He said you and Marshall and your friends would go about it all nice and legal. There wasn't time, Nathan knew. He thought we could be nice and illegal—force Severance to talk, with or without evidence. We got there just as you went in; watched you from across the street. We figured we'd give you a little time to work it out without help. We went up into the hallway outside the apartment. When you yelled, we shot the lock off the door."

Peter looked out at the studio floor where Severance was still continuing painfully with his confession. "You think this will stop them uptown?"

"It could," Knowles said. "But just for now, Styles. You people don't come alive to what we people got to have, and it will be just for now."

"Haven't you learned yet that anarchy doesn't work for anyone?" Peter asked.

"I have given the orders," the Mayor was saying, in a clear, strong voice, "for the troops to withdraw from the boundaries of Harlem. The blocked-off areas around the station here and the station itself will be open to the public again within a half an hour. Trains will run again at the rush hour. General Calhoun's men have been ordered to surrender their arms. I want to tell the people of New York—"

Someone touched Peter on the shoulder. It was Jerry Marshall. He beckoned and Peter followed him out of the control booth into the hall.

"Nice going—and Merry Christmas," Marshall said.

Coming toward them down the hallway was Grace. When she saw Peter she started to run, her hands held out to him.